A 1940s Radio Christmas Carol

Book by
Walton Jones

Music composed and arranged by
David Wohl

Lyrics by
Faye Greenberg

A SAMUEL FRENCH ACTING EDITION

SAMUEL FRENCH

FOUNDED 1830

NEW YORK HOLLYWOOD LONDON TORONTO

SAMUELFRENCH.COM

RENTAL MATERIALS

An orchestration consisting of **Piano/Vocal Score (with optional organ)** will be loaned two months prior to the production ONLY on the receipt of the Licensing Fee quoted for all performances, the rental fee and a refundable deposit. Please note that **bass** and **"sound effect prop" percussion** can be added as desired by the producing group, however no individual scores are available for these parts.

Please contact Samuel French for perusal of the music materials as well as a performance license application.

IMPORTANT BILLING AND CREDIT REQUIREMENTS

All producers of *A 1940s RADIO CHRISTMAS CAROL must* give credit to the Author of the Play in all programs distributed in connection with performances of the Play, and in all instances in which the title of the Play appears for the purposes of advertising, publicizing or otherwise exploiting the Play and/or a production. The name of the Author *must* appear on a separate line on which no other name appears, immediately following the title and *must* appear in size of type not less than fifty percent of the size of the title type.

A non-musical early draft of *A 1940s RADIO CHRISTMAS CAROL* was first produced at Bas Bleu Theatre in Fort Collins, Colorado on November 20, 2007. The performance was directed by Terry Dodd and Wendy Ishii, with sets by Dennis Madigan, costumes by Sandra J. Frye, property design by Michael Gorgan, and lighting by Jimmie Robinson. The production stage manager was Lisa Mason. The cast was as follows:

CLIFTON FEDDINGTON . . . . Bruce Bergquist

DON STERLING . . . . Don Kraus

BARRY MOORE . . . . Rich Hicks

MOE AMBROSE-COHEN . . . . Scott Rathbun

FRITZ CANIGLIARO . . . . Rob Seligmann

JUDY DAVENPORT . . . . Niccole Carner

BUZZ CRENSHAW . . . . Dan Tschirhart

ESTHER LEWIS PIRNIE . . . . Wendy Ishii

FLAPS BENNIGAN . . . . Dick MacDonald

A 1940s RADIO CHRISTMAS CAROL was first produced at Bas Bleu Theatre in Fort Collins, Colorado on November 15, 2008. The performance was directed by Walton Jones and assistant directed by Jessica Lee Rogers, with sets by Dennis Madigan, costumes by Sandra J. Frye, property design by Michael Gorgan, Hair Design by Kirsten Hovorka, and lighting by Dennis Madigan. The production stage manager was Faith Harbert. The cast was as follows:

CLIFTON FEDDINGTON . . . . Michael Stone

WILLIAM ST. CLAIRE . . . . Jonathan Farwell

FRITZ CANIGLIARO . . . . Chris Valcho

CHARLES "CHOLLY" BUTTS . . . . Scott Rathbun

ISADORE "BUZZ" CRENSHAW . . . . Dan Tschirhart

"LITTLE" JACKIE SPARKS . . . . Joshua Savage

MARGIE O'BRIEN . . . . Maggie Tisdale

JUDITH DAVENPORT . . . . Julia Uthe

SALLY SIMPSON . . . . Elizabeth Nodich

ESTHER LEWIS PIRNIE . . . . Wendy Ishii

TOOTS NAVARRE . . . . David Wohl

HAROLD MULLINS . . . . Matt Strauch

CHARACTERS

CLIFTON FEDDINGTON – 55 year-old Mutual Announcer, front man for WOV's Nash-Kelvinator Mystery Theatre. Formerly producer of the "Mutual Manhattan Variety Cavalcade," which Mutual removed from its lineup just after Christmas, 1942. Now broadcasts his Friday night "Man with No Tomorrow" private eye radio drama which originates from a studio near the transmitter in Newark, NJ. A pioneer in "spot advertising." Wears wire-frame glasses like Glenn Miller. Known for being cheap. Has a crush on Judith.

WILLIAM ST. CLAIRE – 70 year-old, retired star of stage and screen with a long list of Broadway credits, 46 films, including the 1916 British film, "The Right to be Happy," aka "Scrooge the Skinflint." With a great mane of dramatic white hair, William is a bit of a curmudgeon and looks down on radio as one of the bastard children of the stage. William's 31 year-old son David served as a pilot in the US Ninth Air Force. His son was killed when his P-47 was shot down over the French city of Toulon in June 1943. Mr. St. Claire, a widower, lives alone on the Upper East Side in Manhattan. He keeps with him a photograph of his son and the telegram that notified him of his son's death. A guest performer in tonight's show, Mr. St. Claire plays Scrooge.

CHARLES "CHOLLY" BUTTS – 35 year-old funny man. Has a day job as a baker at Weequahic Diner (where his specialty is the nesselrode pie). A little stout. Lives in Jersey City, with his wife, Midge, has no kids, and has a hopeless and unrequited crush on Margie. As a regular, plays Mishke Bibble among other cameos.

FRITZ CANIGLIARO – Once an east-coast Florsheim Shoe salesman (and still plugs them whenever he gets an opportunity for a little commission), now a WOV regular, Fritz plays private eye Rick Roscoe, star of Clifton's usual (and very popular) Friday night offering, "The Man with No Tomorrow." Last year, Rick Roscoe had a Christmas show on Christmas Eve (called "Silent Knife, Holy Knife"). Fritz is a little disappointed that the tradition didn't continue. The resident masher, cynic and wise-guy, Fritz plays Frank Nelson cameos in comedy sketches. Always nattily dressed and well-groomed. Wears an Adolph Menjou moustache. In his early 40s.

"LITTLE" JACKIE SPARKS – Not actually "little," but young. A tenor with a high speaking voice. Having just graduated from high school, Jackie, only 17, lives with his mom in suburban Newark. Calls home probably a dozen times a day. Teased a lot. Still has a Sunday paper route. In the winter, wears ear muffs and galoshes. (Think Dennis Day.)

JUDITH DAVENPORT – Although quite the cutup herself, Judith is the resident "leading lady" playing all such roles as a regular. Has two kids and two ex's and wants no more of either. Determined and stubborn. Lives in a brownstone on West 75th Street at Broadway in Manhattan. Considers herself a "legit" actress, Judith has appeared in two New York City stage productions including a role in the chorus of the Mercury Theatre production of "The Cradle Will Rock" four years ago. Day job working as a switchboard operator at Stickel Advertising Agency in Manhattan. Has Clifton's eye. In her 30s.

MARGIE O'BRIEN – Brassy, flippant, with a voice to match (think Ginger Rogers in "Stage Door"). As a show regular, plays the comic roles. This 30 year-old Irish-American comedienne lives with her two sisters, Zazu and Vi, in a two-room apartment in Queens. She works days as a bookkeeper/typist/stenographer/receptionist for William Dougherty, MD, an oculist in Queens. Margie has appeared on countless radio programs, including frequent appearances on the Allen's Alley segment of the Fred Allen Show and is a favorite on The Horn & Hardart Kiddie Hour. Like Cholly, a ham.

SALLY SIMPSON – 20 year-old Sally seems sweet and gentle, but is a tough lady. Lives on the lower east side of Manhattan. As a show regular, plays all animals, babies, insects, little kids. In addition to being a radio personality at WOV, Sally makes the long train ride to Babylon, Long Island, three days a week, to contribute to the war effort by working for Republic Aviation operating drill presses and riveting guns. Sally (whose personal best is 2,155 rivets in one shift) was dubbed "The Home Front Girl" in the company newspaper. Always trying to recruit the other WOV women to join "the cause."

ISADORE "BUZZ" CRENSHAW – His life is his work. The 24 year-old "sound effectician" at WOV. Has a sharp wit and is always agreeable, whistling, and in a good mood. Born and raised in Bayonne where he was valedictorian at Bayonne High, Class of '37. Raised by his Aunts Lulu and Gilly. Moved back to Bayonne when the Cavalcade became Nash Mystery Theater and began broadcasting from Newark. Although he does sound effects for several other shows broadcast by WOV, some in Manhattan, it is clearly Clifton's weekly broadcast that is the biggest challenge and most fun. Wears an FDR button. Spends a lot of time with Sally Simpson. Buzz lives alone.

TOOTS NAVARRE – Musical director, composer and pianist/organist for the Mystery Theatre. (Could be a man or woman.) Besides his/her usual musical chores for WOV, he/she and his/her wife/husband Faldi/Frank provide both underscoring to the radio drama as well as their new and old holiday songs for the broadcast. [Underscoring is left to the discretion of the musical director. The piano and organ are used as contrasting colors, as desired.]

ESTHER LEWIS PIRNIE – backstage audio engineer and transmitter supervisor for WOV Radio. [Optional character. BUZZ can take ESTHER's business and lines, lines in post-show can simply be cut.]

HAROLD J. MULLINS – Concierge of the Hotel Aberdeen in Newark. [Optional character. CLIFTON can take his announcements and business or cut them.]

Note: the characters of **MARGIE** and **JUDITH** could be collapsed into **JUDITH**, as could **FRITZ** be absorbed by the character of **CLIFTON**. As noted above, **ESTHER** and **HAROLD** are optional.

SETTING

WOV-Radio Satellite Studio in the lobby level of the Hotel Aberdeen at 10-12 Washington Place at the foot of Elizabeth Avenue, between Frelinghuysen Avenue and East Peddie Street in Newark, NJ., Bigelow 5-7979.

TIME

Friday, December 24, 1943, 7:30 PM

AUTHOR'S NOTES

Although *A 1940s RADIO CHRISTMAS CAROL* is scored only for keyboards, producers could cast actors who also play instruments to supplement and fill in the orchestrations.

It's worth noting that radio actors frequently used under-the breath ad libs to help coordinate their lines with the sfx. Also, during live radio dramas performers would often drop loose sheets of script onto the floor to avoid the sound of turning pages. Although impractical for the stage, it could be something a few others do which might puzzle St. Claire.

Except where specifically noted, the entire cast is onstage all the time. During the broadcast, their lives, as revealed in the pre- and post-shows (silent behavior or dialogue), continue to be played out for the live audience, things that the radio audience would not see.

A NOTE ON THE MUSIC

Whoever is cast as Toots is encouraged to improvise underscoring, although an indication of underscoring motifs will be provided to those licensing the musical play for performance.

The author will provide free-of-charge the recorded sound effects, pre- and post-show music, reference photos of the period microphones, and a reference DVD video of a 1939 radio drama being performed with actors, microphones, and sound effects men. For these materials, please contact the author at. jones.walton@gmail.com.

A digital mock-up of St. Claire's telegram and the photo of his son, David, the calendar page of December 1943, and the St. Claire poster from a fictitious production of "Macbeth," can also be provided, as well as an example of the "fake" program.

The author wishes to thank Amy Scholl and Steven Adler for their wisdom and advice responding to countless drafts of this script.

(1940s décor randomly tags the studio. Some Christmas decorations, especially around Toots' area, brighten up the institutional green drabness. There is a call board with a few telegrams, phone messages, a pay phone on the wall, sign-in sheets, etc. Magazines and newspapers rest on most surfaces. "On Air," "Applause" and "Laughter" signs hang or are mounted near the ceiling. There is a cathedral radio sitting next to a tall Bunn coffee maker. At present, lights are the unflattering light of work lights. There is a prominent "Currier & Ives" 1943 calendar on the upstage wall, showing the month of December. Days 1-23 are x'ed out. Besides the pay phone, there is a "studio" phone, always answered by Esther Pirnie and off-limits to the cast for placing personal calls.)

(The Feddington players have taken it on the chin over the last year. They are no longer a variety show, as mutual has dumped most of its variety offerings. The studios are a little more crowded, rustic, almost improvised. And they now broadcast from Newark, New Jersey.)

*(Over the house speakers, plays the end of FDR's December 24, 1943 fireside chat. About twenty minutes til curtain, **BUZZ** enters to prepare for the broadcast. He stops to listen occasionally, shakes his head empathically.)*

*(**BUZZ** makes his SFX props ready, makes coffee, sweeps the stage, takes the sacks off of the period mics, and checks all of the cables. The mics have chrome "flags" fixed on the tops and sides that say "WOV" which **BUZZ** polishes carefully. He hauls out the clock, facing it upstage for Clifton to see, after setting the time from his wristwatch. He retrieves a small step ladder from a corner in the studio to open the transome above the door then waving a little air into the studio.)*

(TOOTS is also already there, coming in and out, reading a Life *magazine, and talking sotto voce with* **BUZZ***.)*

(Once they have entered, actors are free to wander around, on and offstage, they enter from the upstage door to the hall or from the "hotel lobby," occasionally shaking styrofoam snow off his or her overcoat, etc. [The stage left or stage right entrance from the theatre lobby should have a door for slamming when characters enter or exit.] Some coats and hats are hung on the coat rack onstage, some are taken offstage. There is a prominent poster of **WILLIAM ST. CLAIRE** *in a Shakespearean production hanging in sight.)*

(The "pre-broadcast" is to be played very quickly, not everything needs to be heard by the audience. And it needs to be played at a pretty fast overlapping clip like the opening scene of "The Front Page")

(Note: "SFX" indicates an effect or anything done by Buzz, the sound effects man. "REC'G" indicates Buzz has "thrown" the needle on a 78-rpm recording on a turntable mounted beside the foley table; "music" refers to a musical bridge or theme provided by **TOOTS** *on the organ and/or piano.)*

FDR VOICE. *(V.O.)* "…We are united in seeking the kind of victory that will guarantee that our grandchildren can grow and, under God, may live their lives, free from the constant threat of invasion, destruction, slavery and violent death."

*(**BUZZ** is putting up a William St. Claire poster.)*

FRITZ. *(entering)* Where's the boss?

*(**BUZZ** "thumbs" offstage.)*

FDR VOICE. *(V.O.)* "Some of our men overseas are now spending their third Christmas far from home. To them and to all others overseas or soon to go overseas, I can give assurance that it is the purpose of their Government to win this war and to bring them home at the earliest possible date."

FRITZ. Coffee ready?

BUZZ. Yep.

FDR VOICE. *(V.O.)* "Tonight, on Christmas Eve, all men and women everywhere who love Christmas are thinking of that ancient town and of the star of faith that shone there more than nineteen centuries ago."

(**CLIFTON** *crosses from the actual lobby door through the door upstage studio.*)

FRITZ. Hey, Clifton.

CLIFTON. *(looking at the poster of St. Claire)* Nice touch, Buzz.

BUZZ. I thought it might make him feel more welcome.

CLIFTON. Buzz, run some audio through that cable by the turntable. I think it's fried.

BUZZ. Right, Mr. Feddington.

(**CLIFTON**, *without stopping, exits through downstage Exit.* **BUZZ** *works on the cable, eventually replacing it.*)

FRITZ. I'm surprised he'd be willing to do this show.

BUZZ. Looking to keep his hand in, I guess.

FRITZ. What's up with the "Mr. Feddington," brownie?

BUZZ. Respect. Something you'd know nothing about.

FRITZ. Hey, be nice. It's Christmas. *(beat)* St. Claire has a son who's over there, yes?

(**FDR VOICE** *continues.*)

BUZZ. *(nodding)* Mm mm.

FRITZ. You know where?

BUZZ. Loose lips…

FRITZ. The best kind.

BUZZ. Loose lips sink ships. *(confidentially)* I think he's a pilot in France somewhere.

FRITZ. *(making coffee)* Mmm, France. Wine. Baguettes. Camembert. And women.

BUZZ. And machine guns, and mortars, and tanks…

(*They listen to* **FDR VOICE.**)

FRITZ. Lighten up, Buzz.

FDR VOICE. *(V.O.)* "American boys are fighting today in snow-covered mountains, in malarial jungles, (and) on blazing deserts, they are fighting on the far stretches of the sea and above the clouds, and fighting for the thing for which they struggle. I think it is best symbolized by the message that came out of Bethlehem."

(After the unintelligible sign-off from an anonymous announcer, the network hosts a generic dance band from some distant city.)

MARGIE. *(entering from upstage door, stomping her feet on the floor mat)* Jeez. What a mess.

BUZZ. *(stops what he's doing, leans on the broom, wistfully)* It's so pretty at first, isn't it? Like when I was a kid, all Currier & Ives. Then the cars turn it into –

CHOLLY. *(entering from theatre lobby, about the snow)* Dreck.

BUZZ. *(not looking up from setting up, sweeping, working)* Cholly Butts.

CHOLLY. *(opening his arms to* **MARGIE***)* Ah, Margie, what a beauty!

FRITZ. Hey, Cholly.

CHOLLY. *(signing in)* Nice drapes, Fritz.

FRITZ. Thanks. *(referring to his shoes)* Check out the kicks.

CHOLLY. Righteous.

MARGIE. Hey, Cholly, How's tricks?

CHOLLY. *(disappointed in her)* Margie, Margie, Margie…it's "nu?"

BUZZ. *(sweeping)* Move, Fritz.

MARGIE. Oh. "Hey Cholly, s'nu?"

CHOLLY. No, no, no. "S'nu"? Just "nu?" And you don't have to say the "Hey Cholly" part. It's all implied in a single "nu".

MARGIE. *(asking again)* "Nu?"

CHOLLY. Yep. And then I say *(with elaborate hand waving)* "E-h-h…"

(She laughs.)

FRITZ. Hey, sweet cheeks.

MARGIE. Put a sock in it, Fritz.

CHOLLY. Oh, that laugh. Without you, Margie, life is a mere bag of shells.

(He goes to give her a peck. She turns so he gets her cheek.)

MARGIE. *(She giggles.)* You're spoken for. And you got flour on your nose.

(She licks her finger and rubs it off. **CHOLLY** *swoons.)*

CLIFTON. *(crossing)* Margie, Cholly.

CHOLLY. Ooo – I'll never wash my nose again.

MARGIE. So how you like the new digs?

CHOLLY. *(waving his hand like earlier)* "E-h-h…" Where's the toilet?

*(***JUDITH** *enters from theatre lobby door.* **CLIFTON** *reenters from upstage door.)*

FRITZ. Judy, I thought you'd never get here.

JUDITH. Judith. And I'm all grown up now, Fritz. I have two kids, two ex's and I'm not looking for any more of either.

BUZZ. *Two* ex's?

JUDITH. It's a "catch and release" program. *(to* **CLIFTON***)* Sally's right behind me. We shared a cab.

*(***SALLY** *enters.)*

Do you know what a cab from Manhattan costs, Clifton?

FRITZ. When are we moving back to the City, Clifton?

CLIFTON. What's wrong with Newark?

FRITZ. *(counting on his fingers)* The air is brown; it smells like a bus station –

SALLY. – and it's 7 bucks from Manhattan; that's what's wrong with Newark.

BUZZ. *(going offstage to wheel out the clock)* Fritz, can you give me a hand?

(**SALLY** *is dressed as the archetypical "Rosie the Riveter."
Her middle two fingers on one hand are taped together
with white tape.* **CHOLLY** *looks at his watch and corrects
the studio clock.*)

JUDITH. Here's a fin.

(*gives* **SALLY** *a five dollar bill*)

Catch you later…

(**JUDITH** *disappears upstage.*)

MARGIE. Unless she's eatin' a potater…

(*Only* **CHOLLY** *laughs.*)

BUZZ. How many rivets today, Sally?

SALLY. Don't work Fridays.

(*Pulling off the tape, trying her fingers.* **BUZZ** *watches.*)

Yesterday, first shift, a little over 1200. (*explaining the
tape*) Trigger finger. (*to* **CLIFTON**) Cliff.

(**BUZZ** *notices the studio clock and readjusts it.*)

You gotta do something about the travel costs. When
I signed on, I knew nothing about the move to Jersey.
I'm almost losing money on this gig.

CLIFTON. I can't help it, Sally; in this economy everybody
has to tighten their belts.

CHOLLY. 'Cept me. I can't tighten mine.

FRITZ. Sally Simpson. How fetching.

SALLY. Go fetch a bone, Fritz.

(**BUZZ** *laughs again.*)

MARGIE. Isn't he awful?

BUZZ. He's Fritz.

SALLY. Gotta go change.

BUZZ. Just wear that for the show.

CHOLLY. Yeah. It's radio.

SALLY. I've got to at least wash up.

CHOLLY. Well, there is that.

SALLY. Hey!

CHOLLY. I'm kidding. You smell like a cinnamon babka.

SALLY. You bring me a pie tonight, Cholly?

CHOLLY. We sold the last piece 15 minutes ago.

BUZZ. To whom?

CHOLLY. *(smiling)* Guilty. *(goes back to reading the Herald Tribune)*

*(**SALLY** laughs, **JUDITH** crosses in front of her.)*

*(to **BUZZ**)* I can't get enough of the stuff. I see it in my sleep. *(rubs his tummy)* 'Tis the season.

*(Silent business. **CHOLLY** notices the studio clock time and "corrects" it, then heads for the phone. This routine can continue throughout the show as long as it's focused. **CLIFTON** exits through upstage door to get new pages and scripts.)*

SALLY. *(brushing her teeth, spitting into Clifton's coffee mug)* Judith, Republic's got a seat on the drill press that's got your name on it.

JUDITH. Are you kidding me? *(laughs)*

SALLY. Come on, Judith. It builds strong bodies eight ways.

JUDITH. I've got a job. And I live in Manhattan.

SALLY. So do I! *(spits again into Clifton's coffee mug)*

*(**TOOTS** is noodling at the piano.)*

CHOLLY. *(holding a period New York City Daily newspaper)* Ah there's bad news tonight!

FRITZ. Yeah, you're here.

ESTHER. *(Appearing suddenly. In productions without Esther, **CLIFTON** should say these lines:)* Cholly, use the pay phone. That's why we got it. The studio phone is only for studio business.

CLIFTON. I know it's odd that we have a phone in the studio, but remember we were lucky to get this room, and the telephone jack was in here so that's where the phone has to be. And anyway, it's Christmas Eve; who's gonna call us anyway? I'm assuming that none of you gave out the number…

(Silence, **CAST** *look around guiltily.)*

ESTHER. Clifton, please remind your cast and crew who makes the business calls at WOV.

CLIFTON. *(grabbing his coffee mug away from* **SALLY***)* You and me, Esther.

ESTHER. *(to* **CHOLLY***)* You see? Him and me. Not him and me and you. Just him and me.

CHOLLY. *(to* **ESTHER***)* Lend me a nickel?

MARGIE. *(bellows)* CLIFF-TONN!!

*(***CLIFTON*** drinks from Sally's toothpaste mug.)*

CLIFTON. *(about the "coffee")* Mm. Minty, full-bodied. Good job on the coffee, Buzz.

BUZZ. Huh?

*(***TOOTS*** exits.)*

MARGIE. Clifton?

CLIFTON. *(to* **MARGIE***)* Yep?

*(***BUZZ*** readjusts the clock.)*

MARGIE. *(flipping through pages)* Aren't we doing the Hobo sketch tonight?

CLIFTON. The only sketch tonight is Christmas Shopping.

MARGIE. *(tossing some script pages up in the air)* Aw, geez.

CHOLLY. *(having dialed the pay phone already)* Hi, Midge, I got here OK. Sure, they're open all night. Clifton, you got a pencil?

MARGIE. *(to* **CLIFTON***)* Lemme see the shopping sketch.

CLIFTON. *(spreading scripts on chairs in piles)* In a minute, soon as I collate them. You're in "Lingerie."

*(***MARGIE*** exits.)*

CHOLLY. *(to* **CLIFTON***, who has given him a pencil)* Margie's in lingerie?
(into phone) Nothing, Midge.

*(***BUZZ*** exits upstage, crossing downstage of* **CHOLLY***, to finish setup.)*

CHOLLY. Okay, what do you want? *(writing)* An order of stuffed cabbage, yeah yeah. The "Weequahic Famous Open Triple-Decker Club Sandwich: corned beef/pastrami/tongue, yeah, sizzling hot off the grill," of course, yeah. Double Russian, yeah-sure. Five half-sours. *(She asks about the Nesselrode pie.)* No we ran out of Nesselrode pie this afternoon. *(defensively)* I did not! No they won't have any more 'til after 10. So how about a slice of the silky-smooth chocolate cream pie? Good choice. Okay. And a basket of hot, soft rolls, of course. *(watches* **MARGIE** *go by)* Okay, Midge. See you after the show.

BUZZ. Hey, Cholly, how's Midge?

CHOLLY. Fat.

JACKIE. *(entering from theatre lobby)* Hey guys, I'm stuck. Can a couple of you give me a hand?

CHOLLY. *(like a "he-man," grabbing his coat)* I got it.

SALLY. No, I got it.

CHOLLY. Come on, you're a girl.

SALLY. Just hold the flashlight.

> *(***CHOLLY*** *and* **SALLY** *exit with* **JACKIE.** **CLIFTON** *looks at* **FRITZ***, who hasn't moved.)*

FRITZ. *(again the new shoes, his excuse for not helping)* Don't want to scuff the new kicks.

> *(***JUDITH** *has re-entered with* **TOOTS** *and heads to the piano with him.* **BUZZ** *has picked up the newspaper Cholly has brought in.)*

CLIFTON. Toots, you finish the verse?

TOOTS. Yep. We're working it right now.

FRITZ. Judith, this song is a career-maker, you know.

> *(***TOOTS** *begins noodling from "Quiet Night.")*

JUDITH. Maybe go right to Broadway?

FRITZ. Or Broad Street.

> *(***JUDITH** *and* **TOOTS** *start rehearsing the ballad at the piano.)*

MARGIE. Aw, quit yer beefin'. Until last year, The Horn and Hardart Kiddie Hour paid me with merchandise. One week I got $8 cash, 2 bottles of Patton Brothers Hair Renew, 11 pounds of bread, and 7 pounds of washers from Henderson's Hardware.

FRITZ. *(privately, to* **JUDITH***)* Hey, I have a something for you. Just a little thing. *(smarmy)* How about drinks after the show?

JUDITH. Fritz. How many times do I have to say "no"?

FRITZ. (*smiling and a little too close to* **JUDITH***)* I love it when you're angry…

CLIFTON. Judith, how about a drink after the show?

JUDITH. You too?

CLIFTON. *(innocently)* What did I say?

FRITZ. I was here first.

SALLY. Clifton, we need to talk about cab fare.

JACKIE. *(having reentered with the rest)* And gas money for all of us who *drive. (He looks at* **SALLY***.)*

MARGIE. You live three blocks from here, squirt.

JACKIE. Hey, it all adds up.

SALLY. But *we* live in Manhattan.

JACKIE. *(smiling)* Hey, Sally, I just got my license.

> **(FRITZ** *and* **CLIFTON** *watch* **JUDITH** *apply stocking lines on the backs of her bare legs with eyebrow pencil.)*

SALLY. *(not impressed)* Great.

BUZZ. Still got the paper route?

JACKIE. *(laughs, then confidentially to* **BUZZ***)* Shhh. Just Sundays.

BUZZ. Watch this.

> **(BUZZ** *folds the newspaper he's been reading in 2.8 seconds, tosses it toward the exit and it lands offstage* **CHOLLY** *calls out.)*

JACKIE. *(humbled)* Wow.

CHOLLY. *(off)* Hey!

(**TOOTS** *plays a fragment of "Take Me Out To The Ballgame."*)

BUZZ. *(proudly)* I won an award.

CHOLLY. *(re-entering)* Hey, Jackie, you missed the porch. *(gives him the newspaper back)* You guys should-a seen Sally lift that rear bumper all by herself!

SALLY. Told you. *(flexes her biceps)*

MARGIE. Wonder Woman.

FRITZ. *(recites the slogan for Wonder Woman comics)* "As beautiful as Aphrodite, as wise as Athena, swifter than Hermes, and stronger than Hercules."

(**BUZZ** *looks at* **FRITZ**, *puzzled.*)

I have a collection.

SALLY. Margie, we could use you on the drill press at Republic.

MARGIE. Yeah? What's it pay?

SALLY. $31.76 a week.

BUZZ. It's on Long Island.

SALLY. You get train fare…

MARGIE. I'd have to quit my job at the oculist's.

CHOLLY. What's an oculist?

MARGIE. I have no idea.

SALLY. Talk to your sisters too. Two million women can't be wrong…

MARGIE. Zazu and Vi don't do well with tools.

CHOLLY. Zazu and Vi??

MARGIE. I didn't name them.

FRITZ. Jackie, what kind of shoes are those?

(**CHOLLY** *watches* **MARGIE** *apply lines on the backs of her legs with eyebrow pencil.*)

JACKIE. Thom McAn's.

FRITZ. Oooo, your poor arches. *(looking around that no one hear this "special deal")* Look, I can get you into a pair of *(showing* **JACKIE** *his)* Florsheims for eight bucks.

JACKIE. But they're rationing shoes now.

FRITZ. I got connections. What are you? 7? 7-1/2?

> (**FRITZ** *goes to the studio phone and begins to dial.*)

ESTHER. *(appears, taking receiver away from him)* That goes for you too, Buster. The studio phone is for business only.

> (*She takes the receiver out of his hand and hangs it up.*)

> (**FRITZ** *gives up and goes to the pay phone to make his call.*)

MARGIE. *(shouting)* CLIFF-TONN!

CLIFTON. I'm right here!

MARGIE. *(flipping through pages)* Hey, we aren't doing the Kindergarten sketch tonight?

CLIFTON. Like I said, we're only doing the shopping sketch.

MARGIE. *(tosses more script pages up in the air)* Aw, geez!

CLIFTON. We can't run long tonight.

MARGIE. Well you cut all my good stuff.

> (**JACKIE** *has been practicing with the newspaper: folding, aiming, throwing.*)

SALLY. Hey fellas, why aren't you working for Uncle Sam?

> (*A pause. Then one by one, the guys put up their hands as they speak.*)

JACKIE. *(holding the newspaper)* Too young.

FRITZ. *(dialing pay phone)* Too old.

CLIFTON. Way too old.

CHOLLY. Flat feet.

> (*All look at* **BUZZ.**)

BUZZ. I enlisted last week.

> (*No one knew.*)

> (*to everyone*) I would've told you all eventually.

SALLY. When do you report?

BUZZ. January 18.

SALLY. When were you planning to tell us?

CHOLLY. Maybe it'll be over by then.

BUZZ. *(half-heartedly)* Yeah.

(pause)

JACKIE. *(putting newspaper back on the coffee table)* Has everyone finished their Christmas shopping?

MARGIE. Jackie!

(studio phone rings)

CHOLLY. A little tact, maybe?

ESTHER. *(holding the receiver of the studio phone)* Jackie, your muthuh. *(hangs up receiver, smiles)* Use the payphone.

FRITZ. *(to* **JACKIE***)* You're all set. New Florsheims next Friday night. Nine bucks.

JACKIE. I thought you said eight.

FRITZ. I get a commission.

JACKIE. Can I borrow a nickel?

FRITZ. Nope.

> *(***JACKIE*** *scours the cast for a nickel, gets one, puts it in the pay phone and dials.)*

CLIFTON. Cholly, the pencil?

FRITZ. Margie, wasn't your beauty mark on the other side last week?

> *(***CHOLLY*** *laughs,* ***MARGIE*** *doesn't think it's funny.)*
>
> *(Eventually everyone is listening to Jackie's phone call home.)*

JACKIE. Hey, Ma. Nope, no skidding. It's just slushy. I got stuck right by the hotel but some of the gang helped me out. You should-a seen Sally; she lifted the whole car. No really, she lifted the whole car. No, I'm not getting a cold. Okay. Okay. Okay.

> *(***TOOTS*** *tinkles something on the piano mocking the tender moment.)*

JACKIE. *(cont.)* *(very quietly)* I love you too. *(even quieter)* Very very. *(beat)* For real. *(beat)* For really real. *(kisses the mouthpiece of the phone)*

(He hangs up, looks around, everyone's staring.)

(innocent) What?

ALL. Awwww.

*(**TOOTS** plays a glissando to punctuate the **CAST** reaction.)*

CLIFTON. How about it, Judith?

JUDITH. What is it with you guys? Depends on the weather. And my cab fare.

FRITZ. How about we all go The Palm after the show?

SALLY. That's a great idea.

CHOLLY. The Palm?

MARGIE. A steakhouse two doors down from the Apollo.

TOOTS. Across the street from the Hotel Theresa.

SALLY. 125th Street.

JACKIE. I can't drive into Manhattan.

FRITZ. We'll take cabs. On Clifton.

CLIFTON. Thanks.

MARGIE. Geez.

JUDITH. Thanks, Clifton.

CLIFTON. Well, I was thinking of something a little quieter.

JUDITH. The Palm is loud, right?

FRITZ. Can't hear yourself think!

JUDITH. Sounds perfect.

FRITZ. The 5 Red Caps, Ivie Anderson, and Oscar Pettiford are joining the Duke tonight. It's better than anything cookin' on 52nd Street.

TOOTS. I'm in.

JUDITH. What time does it start?

TOOTS. Life doesn't start 'til midnight, gang.

BUZZ. I did a broadcast gig there a month ago. They don't even take their instruments out 'til 2.

JACKIE. What does it cost?

BUZZ. I can loan you a couple bucks.

SALLY. You're only seventeen.

CHOLLY. *(glum)* I can't go. I'm delivering a sandwich.

JACKIE. You going, Sally?

CLIFTON. Okay, everyone.

> *(Sudden bustle,* **CLIFTON** *hands out last minute changes to the script, etc. Everyone huddles around* **CLIFTON***, talking at the same time, the audience should not be able to hear specifically what is being said until...)*

> *(Toilet flush offstage.* **CHOLLY** *re-enters.)*

CLIFTON. *(to all but particularly to* **CHOLLY***, entering)* Oh – please don't flush the toilet during the show. The mics will pick it up.

CHOLLY. Check!

CLIFTON. And – good news – the Federal Radio Commission has approved increasing our power to 1000 watts!

> *(The* **CAST** *applauds weakly.)*

FRITZ. Wow. I guess my mom might be able to pick us up now.

CHOLLY. Where does she live?

FRITZ. Across the street.

> *(***CAST*** *laughs.)*

CLIFTON. With the right weather, we'll be up and down the east coast – where you used to sell shoes, Fritz.

FRITZ. Still do.

BUZZ. Where's Mr. St. Claire?

CLIFTON. The car service is bringing him. He'll be here –

ALL. Car service?!

CLIFTON. Back off. We were lucky to sign him. It was the least we could do.

JUDITH. Where's he live?

CLIFTON. Manhattan.

SALLY. He could-a picked us up!

CLIFTON. He's coming from Philadelphia.

FRITZ. Philadelphia?

CLIFTON. Visiting his sister.

CHOLLY. Philadelphia, P.A.

MARGIE. Philadelphia, P.U. *(like "pee yew")*

    (**CHOLLY** *laughs.*)

CLIFTON. The car picked him up at Penn Station at 6:30.

FRITZ. St. Claire's son is overseas right?

CLIFTON. Yes. His son David, uh, was a pilot in the Air Force…

SALLY. Was?

    (**CLIFTON** *lowers and shakes his head.*)

CHOLLY. You're kidding.

CLIFTON. His manager told me.

JUDITH. When?

CLIFTON. June.

MARGIE. *(hands to her mouth)* Oh, God.

    (*There is a pause.*)

FRITZ. How'd it happen?

CLIFTON. He died when his plane went down somewhere over France.

MARGIE. Oh, no.

SALLY. Gee.

    (*pause*)

JACKIE. Anybody know how late Bamberger's is open tonight?

MARGIE & CHOLLY. Jackie!?

    (*beat*)

JACKIE. What? I still need to get something for my girl.

MARGIE. How *is* your mom, Jackie?

    (**CHOLLY** *howls.*)

MARGIE. *(to* **TOOTS***)* Okay, Toots, my turn!

TOOTS. Okay, Margie.

(They do a complete run through of Margie's song.)

(MUSIC: THAT CUTE LITTLE ELF*)*

MARGIE. *(sings)*

I'VE ALWAYS BEEN A NO NONSENSE GAL
DOING WHAT I SHOULD
BUT I'VE TURNED INTO MUSH
SINCE I GOT A CRUSH
AND IT FEELS MIGHTY GOOD
NO MORE SENSIBLE AND SELF RELIANT
THE CHANGE YOU SEE IN ME
IS NOTHING SHORT OF GIANT

THAT CUTE LITTLE ELF SECOND ONE FROM THE RIGHT
WITH EYES THAT SHINE
HE'S FUNNY AS HECK, AND HE'S PRINCELY POLITE
HANDS OFF HE'S MINE
THE DRAPE OF HIS SUIT, THAT FABULOUS HAT
WHO WOULDN'T LOOK UP TO A GUY LIKE THAT
BOY OH BOY, WHAT A SIGHT
THAT CUTE LITTLE ELF SECOND ONE FROM THE RIGHT

THAT FUN LOVING ELF SECOND ONE FROM THE RIGHT
ONE OF THE SWELLS
A STYLE ALL HIS OWN THAT IS BOUNCY AND BRIGHT
HIS SHOES HAVE BELLS
HE LIKES SHOOTING DARTS, AND PLAYING CROQUET
OR TO RIDE BY MY SIDE IN A ONE HORSE SLEIGH
JUMPIN' JIVE AND HOLD TIGHT
THAT FUN LOVING ELF SECOND ONE FROM THE RIGHT

HE LABORS DAY AND NIGHT
HELPING JOLLY MR. C
BUT HE'S MAMA'S LITTLE HELPER
WHEN HE'S SNUGGLING HERE WITH ME
HE WRAPS A PERFECT GIFT
WITH FINE RIBBONS AND A BOW
BUT HE'S BETTER AT UNWRAPPING
TRUST ME, I KNOW
I KNOW

MARGIE. *(cont.)*

> I WANT THAT CUTE LITTLE ELF SECOND ONE FROM THE
>   RIGHT
> AND I WON'T QUIT!
> I FOUND ME AN ELF WITH A BIG APPETITE
> WE'RE A PERFECT FIT
> I LOVE HIS SWEET, POINTY EARS, THAT BOISTEROUS LAUGH
> MY DREAM IS TO MAKE HIM MY BETTER HALF
> THIRTY-SIX INCHES OF SHEER DELIGHT
> THAT CUTE LITTLE ELF SECOND ONE FROM THE RIGHT
>
> *(All applaud spontaneously.)*

MARGIE. Just before intermission, right, Clifton?

CLIFTON. That's right, Margie.

MARGIE. Hot dog!

> **(HAROLD** *has entered with a small theatrical trunk
> that carries St. Claire's stock properties and costumes.*
> **WILLIAM ST. CLAIRE** *enters. There is a pause and,
> slowly, one by one, everyone looks at him. His shocks
> of long white hair are classically dramatic. He wears a
> cape.* **HAROLD** *exits.)*

FRITZ. *(rushing to meet him, shaking his hand)* Mr. St. Claire, it is such a privilege. I'll be doing Marley and Christmas Present.

ST. CLAIRE. *(putting his hat in* **FRITZ**'s *outstretched hand)* Will you take my coat and hat?

> **(FRITZ** *takes St. Claire's coat, hat, gloves, etc. to the coat
> rack.)*

BUZZ. Mr. St. Claire, I am the sound effectician here at WOV. I saw your "Hamlet" when I was a little boy.

ST. CLAIRE. You must have been very little indeed.

> **(JUDITH** *approaches the old actor, she shakes his hand—
> she speaks in her best mid-Atlantic accent.)*

JUDITH. Mr. St. Claire, I am Judith Davenport. I'll be playing Bella, and Mrs. Cratchit in tonight's performance.

CHOLLY. *(to* **MARGIE***)* What's that accent?

JACKIE. *(takes* **ST. CLAIRE**'s *hand)* Hey, John Sparks, and I play Young Scrooge and Tiny Tim.

MARGIE. *(to* **CHOLLY**) *John* Sparks?

*(***JACKIE*** shushes* **MARGIE**.*)*

SALLY. I play all the kids. And dogs, animals, bugs…and the spooky stuff.

CHOLLY. Bob Cratchit, and any ethnic characters.

MARGIE. I do Christmas Past and all things funny.

CHOLLY. Can we get you anything, Mr. St. Claire? Coffee? Tea? Water?

FRITZ. *(making a joke)* Scotch?

ST. CLAIRE. *(looks around, sizing up the cast)* Water only, please. Hot, but not too hot, with a slice of lemon and a drip or two of honey.

SALLY. We were so saddened to hear about your son.

ST. CLAIRE. Mm?

MARGIE. How're you holding up?

ST. CLAIRE. I miss him.

JACKIE. Sally makes P-47s in Long Island.

CHOLLY. *(scolding him)* Jackie.

ST. CLAIRE. David pilots a P-47.

SALLY. *(with raised eyebrows)* He does. *(haltingly)* Well, then he should be fine. Those P-47s are fine aircraft. And safe. Too. I mean, I know them inside and out. So…

ST. CLAIRE. I need a little quiet now to prepare for my performance.

CLIFTON. *(shouting toward the theatre lobby door)* OK, Harold, let 'em in.

(A mêlée of commotion and last minute warmups. **MARGIE** *is finishing her nails, some effect props have spilled onto the floor and* **BUZZ** *and* **SALLY** *are straightening them up, while…)*

*(***HAROLD**, *with little enthusiasm, recites a litany of rules to an invisible audience; entering,* **TOOTS** *warms up, as well.)*

CLIFTON. Ladies and gentlemen, please have your tickets out. Petie, Dottie, and Miss Crabtree will direct you to your seats. Please, no smoking in the studio, it craps up the audio equipment and the butts burn the carpet. Spanky will be happy to assist anyone who needs a cab after the broadcast. Enjoy the show.

JACKIE. *(stumbles through articulation exercises,* SALLY *laughs)* "The seething sea ceaseth, and having ceaseth, the seething sea sufficeth me."

ST. CLAIRE. *(to* JACKIE*)* Shoo, boy.

FRITZ. *(about St. Claire to* CLIFTON*)* Bah, humbug.

*(*JACKIE *crosses downstage of* CHOLLY*, as he passes,* CHOLLY *is coaching* MARGIE *on all things Yiddish.)*

CHOLLY. No, it's got the guttural thing going, say "chutz-pah"
[PRON. "CH" AS IN THE SCOTTISH WORD "LOCH"]

MARGIE. Hoots-spa.

*(*CHOLLY *keeps trying.* JUDITH *sings full-out and* TOOTS *accompanies.)*

(Continued bustle. Last minute push to get ready. In contrast, ST. CLAIRE *moves very slowly, sits patiently, script closed and resting on his knees, completely prepared. He watches the entertainment with some disdain.* CAST *go into the house and hand out the "fake" programs with the characters' bios and broadcast information.)*

(As show time approaches, CLIFTON *heads for the center mic.)*

(SFX: BUZZ *CRASHES A PAIR OF BAND CYMBALS)*

(With the crash of Buzz's cymbals, all is still and the lights suddenly shift to performance lights.)

CLIFTON. *(to the audience)* Good evening to you, ladies and gentlemen of our studio audience. *(SILENCE)* We'll be on the air in just a few minutes. I'd like to take this opportunity to welcome you as our studio audience tonight. Now folks, a word from the Concierge of the Hotel Aberdeen. Mr. Harold Mullins. Harry?

HAROLD. Harold.

CLIFTON. Harold.

HAROLD. *(with even less enthusiasm)* Ladies and gentlemen, the buses will leave from the Elizabeth Avenue entrance of the hotel at half-past 10 tonight. These are the last busses that will depart the Weequahic *[pron. we-KWAY-ik, or, for locals, we-KWAYK]* area of Newark tonight. We at the Aberdeen, however, recommend that you avoid the dangerous trip home tonight and take advantage of the deluxe accommodations we have available tonight at the Aberdeen, the pride of Newark, New Jersey. Just stop by the front desk during the show or at intermission. Although our dining services will be closed by that time, the Weequahic Diner is open all night.

CHOLLY. ...and the nesselrode pie is especially good tonight.

FRITZ. He ought to know.

MARGIE. He makes 'em.

CHOLLY. *(shy smile)* Every day.

MARGIE. *(rubbing* **CHOLLY***'s tummy)* ...and eats 'em.

CHOLLY. *(still smiling)* ...every night.

HAROLD. *(clears his throat loudly)* Our ensemble is passing out your free souvenir program *(he holds one up)* in which you can read about the cast and tonight's performance. We would like to also take this time to welcome the members of the *(reading from a large index card he removes from the inside pocket of his suit coat)* "Order of the Mystic Shrine" who are conventioning here at the Aberdeen. *(as he puts the card back into the pocket)* We applaud the Shriners' outstanding War Bond sales record and the lead they take in Civil Defense work in all of our communities.

CLIFTON. Yes, the Shriners are a most serious and dedicated group.

CHOLLY. *(mockingly)* You betcha!

(MUSIC: STUPID ORGAN GAMESHOW STING)

CLIFTON. No, Toots, I am not forgetting you! What would our show be without Toots Navarre and our new Hammond "B"! Thank you, Toots.

TOOTS. You can call me Toots.

CLIFTON. Thank you…Toots.

TOOTS. Soli-tudy.

> *(**ESTHER PIRNIE** slips onstage wearing her signature overalls, stringing a cable from offstage over to Buzz's turntable.)*

CLIFTON. Oh – and let's not forget the gal who makes this all happen, without whom none of us would be here tonight…our technical wizard and transmission goddess, Miss Esther Lewis Pirnie!

ESTHER. Everybody, the studio phone is for official business *only*. For the *personal* stuff *(gestures to it and smiles)* – we got a pay phone.

CLIFTON. …Thanks, Esther. Keep 1280 kilocycles clear and strong for our show.

ESTHER. *(Sees the studio audience. Locks up, paralyzed by stage fright.)* Okay. *(She sneaks offstage.)*

BUZZ. *(off-mic)* 35 seconds…

CLIFTON. Thank you, Buzz. Now folks, when you see the "On Air" signs flash…

> *(SFX: ON AIR SIGNS FLASH)*

BUZZ. *(off)* 30 seconds. Places, everyone.

> *(Cast take their places watching **BUZZ** for the countdown. **MARGIE** is waving her nails to dry them.)*

CLIFTON. …we will be broadcasting live tonight, Christmas eve, 1943, courtesy of WOV broadcasting from our shiny new broadcast towers here in beautiful downtown Newark.

BUZZ. Stand by.

Now folks, in their efforts to support our men and women in the armed forces, the War Department has provided broadcast studios like ours with the equipment necessary to produce this program on what is known as a "V-Disc."

(**BUZZ** *gestures to a sign in front of the machine that says "Supplied by the music branch of the Special Services division of the military. Victory disk lathe and shellac disks property of the War Department.")*

This enterprise is only 3-months old but, with it, our boys overseas can enjoy the very same Merry Christmas as you in home town America.

(**BUZZ** *puts a shellac disk on the v-disk lathe and puts the needle down.)*

And of course, you know what to do when you see these signs flash…

(SFX: APPLAUSE SIGNS FLASH)

CLIFTON. Ah, I knew you'd know what to do.

BUZZ. Standby.

CLIFTON. Thank you, Buzz.

BUZZ. In 5…4…3…

(holds up two fingers, then one finger, pointing to **CLIFTON***)*

(REC'G: TIME TONE)

CLIFTON. *(official)* This is the Mutual Broadcasting System. *(simply)* It's 8 o'clock, Eastern War Time.

(MUSIC: INTRO TO OPENING SONG)

(high-power) Live from the lobby of the beautiful Hotel Aberdeen at 10-12 Washington Place in lovely Newark, New Jersey, WOV is on the air!

(SFX: APPLAUSE SIGN FLASHES)

(Lights have shifted to the saturated, rich and colorful lights of the broadcast. **CAST** *surrounds microphones.)*

(MUSIC: NEWARK*)*

CLIFTON & COMPANY *(sings)*

WHAT DO YOU DO
WHEN YOU NEED EXCITEMENT?
WHERE CAN YOU GO
WHEN YOU NEED A THRILL?
THERE'S ONE PLACE I KNOW
WHERE THE LAUGHTER COMES EASY
YOUR PULSE STARTS TO RACE
AND YOUR FEET WON'T STAY STILL
NOBODY LEAVES FEELIN' DOWN
YOU'LL GO NUTS FOR THIS SWINGIN' TOWN

IT'S TRUE, BLUE, NEW, NEW
NEWARK
N-E-W-A-R-K *(SPELL IT)*
THAT'S RIGHT, NEW, NEW, NEW, NEW
NEWARK
IT'S EASY TO SPELL
DELIGHTFUL TO SAY
OH, YOU, YOU, YOU, YOU
NEWARK
YOU ARE THE ESSENCE OF CLASS
BREATHE IN THE BANKS OF THE MIGHTY PASSAIC
NEWARK, YOU'RE A GAS!

THE MOUNTAINS OF NEWARK
THE WATER FOUNTAINS OF NEWARK
AND NARY A CLOUD UP ABOVE
THE GLAMOUR OF NEWARK
CRAZY CLAMOR OF NEWARK
AND EVERY LAST NEWARKIAN
IS CHOCK FULL OF LOVE
IT'S HEAVEN ON EARTH
AND IT NEVER WILL SPOIL
THAT'S WHY WHEN I DIE
JUST PLANT ME IN THE NEWARK SOIL

NEW, NEW, NEW, NEW
NEWARK,
A STAR SPANGELED HOLIDAY
HALLELU, LU, LU, LU

NEWARK
JUST SEEIN' THE SITES
CAN MAKE YOU FEEL GAY
OH, YOU, YOU, YOU, YOU
NEWARK
YOU'RE A HUMDINGER, IT'S TRUE
NEW YORK IS SWELL BUT IT JUST AIN'T NO "JERSEY"
    NEWARK, PRIDE OF THE RED, WHITE & BLUE
N-E-W-A-R-K
NEW JERSEY, U S A.
(SFX: APPLAUSE SIGNS FLASH)

CLIFTON. Thank you, ladies and gentlemen. Celebrating our beautiful new home here in the garden spot of the Garden State: Newark, New Jersey. That was Toots Navarre and the Boutonnieres!

(SFX: APPLAUSE SIGNS FLASH)

(dramatically) Tonight…

(MUSIC: LOW DRAMATIC BASS)

(unctuous and scary, with a sneer) The Nash-Kelvinator Mystery Theatre. Brought to you by Nash. "Nash is here to stay."

(MUSIC: MUSIC BUILDS, CUTS OUT)

*(**MARGIE** takes out her gum, puts it on top of the microphone nearest to Toots…)*

(SFX: GUN SHOT FROM STARTERS PISTOL [MICS OFF FOR THIS AND THE SCREAM])

*(…**MARGIE** screams, takes back her gum and matter-of-factly walks back to her chair while chewing it.))*

(MUSIC: CONTINUES, LOW, SUSPENSEFUL TONES)

CLIFTON. Yes, the Nash-Kelvinator Mystery Theatre, your weekly departure to mystery and adventure. Tonight, we present…

(MUSIC: SUDDEN SHIFT TO A CHEERY AND LIGHT INSTRUMENTAL OF "DECK THE HALLS")

…the seasonal classic, Charles Dickens' "A Christmas Carol."

CLIFTON. Hi folks, it's Clifton Feddington.

(SFX: APPLAUSE SIGNS FLASH)

Thank you, folks, thank you. *(humbly)* You're so *very* kind.

And of course thanks to you folks at home and overseas. Thank you for spending another Friday night with your friends at WOV.

Our regular programming...

(MUSIC: TOOTS PLAYS "FILM NOIR" THEME [MINOR KEY])

...the hard-boiled detective Rick Roscoe in "The Man with No Tomorrow" will return next Friday *(FRITZ waves)*, and although last year's episode of the Rick Roscoe Christmas thriller, "Silent Knife, Holy Knife" was a great success –

(FRITZ "stabs" at an invisible opponent.)

(MUSIC: SEGUE AS ONE INTO "DECK THE HALLS")

 – we hope to start a new holiday tradition tonight with our freshly contemporary retelling of Dickens' Christmas classic, "A Christmas Carol."

(MUSIC: OUT)

Now how could anyone imagine "A Christmas Carol" without the resounding "Bah Humbug" of Ebenezer Scrooge! We are privileged and humbled to introduce you to the star of stage and screen, William St. Claire.

(SFX: APPLAUSE SIGNS FLASH)

Welcome to WOV New Jersey Studios, Bill.

ST. CLAIRE. That's William.

(CLIFTON marks the correct pronunciation with his everpresent pencil. CLIFTON gestures to audience for more applause.)

(SFX: APPLAUSE SIGNS FLASH)

(ST. CLAIRE bows humbly from the waist.)

ST. CLAIRE. Thank you.

CLIFTON. And a very Merry Christmas to you, William.

ST. CLAIRE. You'll excuse me if I don't respond in kind but I'm not much of a "holiday" person.

CLIFTON. *(minor setback)* Well…

FRITZ. *(to* **CHOLLY**, *quietly off-mic but still audible)* Bah, humbug.

CLIFTON. Well, it must be a very different experience performing in radio, William.

ST. CLAIRE. I'll let you know.

CLIFTON. After years on the stage and on the silver screen –

ST. CLAIRE. – this is more than a little step down.

CLIFTON. *(unflappable)* So this your first radio appearance?

ST. CLAIRE. Appearance?

CLIFTON. I meant to say will this be your first radio performance?

ST. CLAIRE. It will, yes. I have appeared on Broadway twenty-one times and I have made over forty films, but this is my first flight on the air, so to speak.

CLIFTON. *(a tiny setback)* Well, we hope you enjoy it as much as I know we will –

ST. CLAIRE. And, speaking of flight, I am thrilled that this show is being broadcast to the men and women in the armed forces. As you know, my son David pilots a P-47 for the US Ninth Air Force and I would like to send a personal greeting to him at this time.

CLIFTON. *(a little thrown)* Of course. *(steps back)*

ST. CLAIRE. David, I love you and am so very proud of what you are doing for our country. But I cannot celebrate Christmas properly until you return home, so please come home soon.

*(**CAST** is a little bewildered by St. Claire's message to his son who the cast knows has died.)*

(SFX: APPLAUSE SIGNS FLASH)

*(**CLIFTON** cues **JACKIE**. **ST. CLAIRE** sits down and sips his water.)*

JACKIE. Say, Mr. Feddington?

(MUSIC: BRIEF TINKLING)

CLIFTON. Little Jackie Sparks, ladies and gentlemen.

(SFX: APPLAUSE SIGNS FLASH)

JACKIE. Before we get started with tonight's broadcast…

CLIFTON. Yes?

JACKIE. Well, it's Christmas Eve and all, and I haven't bought my mom a present yet!

CLIFTON. Jackie, you do this every Christmas. When will you learn to shop early?

JACKIE. I know…

CLIFTON. I'll tell you what Jackie, let's you and I go right now. I have to pick up a few things too.

MARGIE. Hey could I go too?

CLIFTON. Margie O'Brien everyone!

(SFX: APPLAUSE SIGNS FLASH)

Sure. Come on along. While we go next door to Bingles Department Store, why don't Toots and The Boutonnieres sing a Christmas carol or two?

JACKIE. That's a swell idea, Cliff.

CLIFTON. Toots?

*(MUSIC: **TOOTS**, OUT FRONT WITH HIS BATON, CONDUCTS THE COMPANY SINGING "DECK THE HALLS.")*

COMPANY. *(sings)*
DECK THE HALLS WITH BOUGHS OF HOLLY
FA LA LA LA LA LA LA LA LA
TIS THE SEASON TO BE JOLLY
FA LA LA LA LA LA LA LA LA
DON WE NOW OUR GAY APPAREL
FA LA LA LA LA LA LA LA LA
TROLL THE ANCIENT YULE TIDE CAROL
FA LA LA LA LA LA LA LA LA

(SFX: SALVATION ARMY BELL, CROSSFADES WITH:)

(REC'G: DEPARTMENT STORE CROWDS)

FRITZ. Now, through the magic of radio, we find ourselves in Bingle's Department Store amidst the mad Christmas Eve rush.

(SFX: DEPARTMENT STORE DOOR AND "DING DING" FROM DEPARTMENT STORE. A CROWD OF SHOPPERS.)

(Note: the pace of the shopping sketch is quick. Build to laughs, then pause expectantly. Build to the presumptive laughs indicated as with (L) below.)

(SFX: LAUGHTER SIGN FLASHES WITH EVERY "L" INDICATED.)

JUDITH. *(pinching her nose so she'll sound like she's on a public address system)* Attention, shoppers: 2-for-1 Sale in "Lingerie," 2-for-1 Sale in "Lingerie." That's a 2-for-1 Sale in "Lingerie."

CLIFTON. Well, here we are. Gee, it's crowded in here. Everybody pushing and shoving. Give me your hand, Margie.

JUDITH. *(moving to the Downstage mic, a club lady)* Let go of me, young man. My name's Bertha. *(L)*

CLIFTON. Oh, pardon me, Madame. Margie, Margie where are you?

MARGIE. *(talking into a cereal box)* I'm over here in "Lingerie."

CLIFTON. Well, take it off and stick with me. *(L)* Jackie, meet us back here in a few minutes.

JACKIE. Okay, Mr. Feddington.

CLIFTON. Oh Margie, I need you to help me pick something out for Judith.

MARGIE. Okay, but what about me?

CLIFTON. Santa'll take care of you.

MARGIE. That's what you said last year and that rabbit muff was still moving. *(L)*

CLIFTON. I think I'll get her something in the jewelry department.

MARGIE. Good idea.

CLIFTON. Now I wonder where the jewelry counter – oh, mister…

FRITZ. *(as Frank Nelson)* Y-e-e-e-e-s.

CLIFTON. Is this the jewelry counter?

FRITZ. No, I'm a deep sea diver and these are my pearls. *(L)*

CLIFTON. I'd like to buy a lady's wristwatch.

FRITZ. How about a nice fountain pen?

CLIFTON. I don't want a fountain pen, I want a wristwatch.

FRITZ. How are you gonna write a letter with a wristwatch? *(L)*

CLIFTON. Now look, you, I don't want to write a letter!

FRITZ. You don't, eh?

CLIFTON. No.

FRITZ. Well it's guys like you that cause all the trouble in this country.

CLIFTON. What trouble? Look, you wanna sell me a wristwatch or not?

FRITZ. I wouldn't sell you a wristwatch if you were John Cameron Swayze. *(L)*

CLIFTON. Come on, Margie, let's go.

MARGIE. Why don't you just take the fountain pen, Cliff. I think Judith would love it.

CLIFTON. All right. How much is the fountain pen?

FRITZ. Four dollars.

CLIFTON. All right. Here you are. Wrap it up and I haven't got all day.

FRITZ. Okay.

CLIFTON. Fresh guy.

(SFX: PAPER CRUNCHING)

CLIFTON. Hey, what's the idea wrapping that pen in a blotter?

FRITZ. It leaks a little. *(L)*

CLIFTON. Four dollars for a leaky pen; I oughta report you. What's your name?

FRITZ. Woo-Woo Smith. *(L)*

CLIFTON. Gimme back my four dollars.

MARGIE. Come on, Cliff. Hey, look:
there's Santy Claus over there, sitting in that sleigh.

JACKIE. Jeez, all dressed up in red.

CLIFTON. Let's go over and see 'em. He looks so fat and jolly.

(**CHOLLY** *takes issue with the fat comment.*)

Come on, let's go talk to 'em.

MARGIE. *(giggles)* This oughta be fun.

JACKIE. I'm scared.

CLIFTON. *(having a good time already)* Funny, I feel just like a kid again.

MARGIE. Go ahead, talk to him, Cliff.

CLIFTON. Oh, I don't wanna. He might ask me if I've been a good boy.

MARGIE. Oh, go on, Cliff.

CLIFTON. Hello, Santy Claus.

CHOLLY. *(as old Mishke Bibble, speaking with a heavy "Yiddish" accent)* Hello, stranger! *(L)*

(*SFX: APPLAUSE SIGNS FLASH*)

CLIFTON. Hey, it's Mishke Bibble!

CHOLLY. No, I'm Kris Kringle now.

CLIFTON. How have you been, Meesh?

CHOLLY. Oh, life is one long trip to the toilet. *(L)*

CLIFTON. Well, tell me Meesh. How do you happen to be Santy Claus?

CHOLLY. I don't know. I came in here to buy a suit and they sold me a red one. *(L)*

CLIFTON. It is kinda loud, Mishke.

CHOLLY. I feel like a stop light. *(L)*

CLIFTON. How do you like talking to all the little children?

CHOLLY. Well, I guess it's better than a trip to the dentist. *(L)* Tell me, Margie, what do *you* want for Christmas?

MARGIE. Can you put a mink coat in my stocking?

CHOLLY. For you, Margie, I'd put anything in your stocking.

MARGIE. Boy, you *are* Santy Claus.

CLIFTON. Jackie, tell Santy what *you* want.

JACKIE. Oh, I'm too big for that stuff.

CHOLLY. Oh, tell me Jackie boychik, what would you like to find in your stocking Christmas morning?

JACKIE. Me. My feet are cold. *(L)*

CHOLLY. Not too bright. Ever try milking him? *(L)*

CLIFTON. Well, Meesh, we gotta be getting back to the station. When will I see you again?

CHOLLY. Well I'll tell you, Cliff:

(MUSIC: INTRO TO "COMIN' ROUND THE MOUNTAIN")

CHOLLY. *(sings)*
> I'LL BE COMING DOWN YOUR CHIMNEY WHEN I COME
> I'LL BE COMING DOWN YOUR CHIMNEY WHEN I COME

CLIFTON. *(sings)*
> YOU'LL BE COMING DOWN MY CHIMNEY

MARGIE. *(sings)*
> HE'LL BE COMING DOWN HIS CHIMNEY

CHOLLY. *(sings)*
> I'LL BE COMING DOWN WHEN SMOKE GETS IN MY EYES

MARGIE & JACKIE. *(sing)*
> HE'LL BE COMIN DOWN CLIFF'S CHIMNEY WHEN HE –

CHOLLY. *(speaking quickly in tempo)*
> CAN'T YOU HEAR ME CALLING WHEN THE SNOW IS GENTLY FALLING?

MARGIE & JACKIE. *(sing)*
> HE'LL BE COMING DOWN THE CHIMNEY WHEN HE COMES

CHOLLY. *(speaking in tempo)*
> I WOULD LIKE A CUPPA TEA WHEN I BEND YOU ON MY KNEE

ALL. *(sing)*
> HE'LL BE COMING DOWN THE CHIMNEY; HE'LL BE COMING DOWN THE CHIMNEY

CHOLLY. *(sings)*

I'LL BE COMING DOWN YOUR CHIMNEY WHEN I...

*(***TOOTS*** *lifts his hands to play a big final chord;* ***CHOLLY*** *continues, "improvising.")*

AH-H-H-H-H-H-H

*(***TOOTS*** *lifts his hands again to play a big final chord;* ***CHOLLY*** *continues, "improvising.")*

CHIM-I-NEY, CHIM-I-NEY, CHIM-I-NEY, CHIM-I-NEY, CHIM-I-NEY, CHIM-I-NEY, CHIM-I-NEY, CHIM-I-NEY. FIGARO, FIGARO, FIGARO, FIGARO, FIGARO, FIGARO. FIGARO, FIGARO, FIGARO.

(laughs and cries like Pagliacci)

COME.

CLIFTON. See you later, Mishke. Come on, kiddies, we got a show to do!

(SFX: APPLAUSE SIGNS FLASH)

(MUSIC: REPRISE OF "CHIMNEY...")

(Studio phone rings. ***ESTHER PIRNIE*** *slips onstage and answers it. She signals* ***JACKIE***.*)*

ESTHER. Jackie, your mutha. *(hangs up, smiles)* Use the pay phone.

*(***JACKIE*** *excuses himself. Others laugh.)*

CLIFTON. Thank you, ladies and gentlemen, we are beginning our own Christmas tradition tonight with our first annual radio production of Charles Dickens' "A Christmas Carol." You know folks, it was 100 years ago this week when Mr. Charles Dickens completed his timeless Christmas classic, "A Christmas Carol." It was the week of December 19, 1843.

*(***JACKIE*** *re-enters. Noises, people talking, laughing from the theatre lobby.)*

And it has taken this long to find its way to us at WOV and to the Feddington Players. And we've added a few surprises to the story and...

(Still, from the theatre lobby, loud revelling, party horns and clackers, laughter builds until it is impossible to continue. **HAROLD** *has entered.* **CAST** *moves closer to theatre lobby door to see what's up.)*

(NOISES UNDER)

CLIFTON. Of course, you'll meet all of your favorite WOV characters, too, who will help us present to you the most popular and enduring Christmas story of all time. *(finally)* Harold, what *is* that?

CHOLLY. I'll bet it's the Shriners.

HAROLD. *(wearing a fez, loudly)* The Shriners just got back from their Christmas Parade.

CLIFTON. Well, get rid of them.

CHOLLY. Told you.

*(***HAROLD*** *exits. The unmistakeable revelling continues, then stops suddenly.)*

(MUSIC: BRIDGE AND UNDER)

CLIFTON. And now, "A Christmas Carol," by Charles Dickens, brought to you by Nash-Kelvinator. Chapter One, Marley's Ghost.

(MUSIC: THEME)

NARRATOR (CLIFTON). Marley was dead to begin with – in fact, old Marley couldn't be deader. These days he lies six feet underground keeping company with worms and maggots. But tonight, Christmas Eve...Scrooge is in for the surprise of his miserable life.

Marley was Scrooge's partner so many years ago and Scrooge is now the sole proprietor of Scrooge & Co.

(MUSIC: "GOD REST YE MERRY GENTLEMEN")

(SFX: CARRIAGES, HORSES CLIP CLOPPING)

*(***TOOTS*** *can't find his baton and so conducts with a candy cane.* **CAST** *laughs while they sing.)*

CAST. *(sings)*
> GOD REST YE MERRY, GENTLEMEN
> LET NOTHING YOU DISMAY
> REMEMBER, CHRIST, OUR SAVIOUR
> WAS BORN ON CHRISTMAS DAY
> TO SAVE US ALL FROM SATAN'S POWER
> WHEN WE WERE GONE ASTRAY
> O TIDINGS OF COMFORT AND JOY,
> COMFORT AND JOY
> O TIDINGS OF COMFORT AND JOY

(They continue the second verse ooo-ing, under.)

NARRATOR. *(under)* Old Scrooge is a money-lender, a collector who sits busy in his counting-house, day in, day out, counting and re-counting other people's money from which he takes a substantial share, always keeping a watchful eye on his clerk, Bob Cratchit, who counts huge piles of coins by the light of one teenie weenie candle, and scratches the figures in the ledger.

FRITZ. *(off-mic)* Teenie weenie?

(SFX: COIN AND PAPER MONEY COUNTING, SRATCHING QUILL ON PAPER)

BOB CRATCHIT (CHOLLY). *(to himself)* …two hundred and nineteen, twenty, twenty-one, twenty-two, one, two, carry the two… *(sings along)* "God rest ye merry gentlemen, let nothing you dismay…" *(to himself)* …two hundred twenty-three, twenty-six, twenty-nine, naught, naught, carry the naught… *(sings)* "…on Christmas Day!…" *(to himself)* …two hundred thirty-one, seventeen more, that's two hundred forty-eight –

SCROOGE. *(suddenly and loudly, he has put on his half-glasses)* Cratchit!

CRATCHIT. *(with a start)* Ooo.

(SFX: STACKS OF COINS FALL TO FLOOR)

CRATCHIT. Er, yes, sir, Mr. Scrooge?

SCROOGE. Now look what you've done, you dolt. If you did your job without making that horrible holiday warbling, I'll bet you wouldn't make mistakes like that. *(with a smile)* I guess you're going to have to start all over again, now won't you?

CRATCHIT. It's just that it's…it's Christmas Eve and, well, there's almost no candle left –

SCROOGE. I knew it! Same old story…Every year. And I suppose you'll want the entire day off tomorrow?

CRATCHIT. *(haltingly)* If it's quite convenient, sir.

SCROOGE. *(really unpleasant)* Well it's *not* convenient – it's anything *but* convenient!

CRATCHIT. Ummm…

SCROOGE. *(giving in)* Well, you'll be no use to me if I kept you here. Alright, tonight and tomorrow, but I'll have to dock your wages…

CRATCHIT. Well, sir, I –

SCROOGE. Oh – you think I should pay you even when you don't work?! What, are you drunk? A little too much mulled wine today, Cratchit?!

CRATCHIT. It's only this once, sir.

SCROOGE. No, this happens every year, Cratchit. *(mocking him)* "Please, Mr. Scrooge, I wouldn't ask if this weren't Christmas Eve." Bah! Humbug! Alright, you can have tomorrow off and you can leave early tonight but I want to see you sitting at that desk no later than 3 A.M. on the 26th, you understand?!

(SFX: **CRATCHIT** *SCURRYING TO READY TO LEAVE AND LEAVING WHILE TALKING)*

CRATCHIT. *(wrapping himself in mimed coat, muffler, cap)* Oh, I will, sir. Just let me get off my stool now and get on my coat and scarf *(mimed with accompanying sound effects)*.

(SFX: **SALLY** *MOVES HER STOOL,* **BUZZ** *DOES THE CLOTHING)*

I'll be here sir. You can count on me. 3 A.M. sharp. Even earlier maybe. And I'll have your tea ready for you, sir. Thank you, sir. Thank you.

(SFX: DOOR OPENS)

CRATCHIT. Yes, sir. Good night, sir.

(steps away from the mic, as if in a doorway, turns back)

And Merry Christmas to you, sir.

SCROOGE. *(sweetly)* Good night, Cratchit!

(SFX: DOOR CLOSES)

(laughs) You fool. *(mocking him)* "And Merry Christmas to you, sir." Humbug! *(laughing to himself)* I, on the other hand, I have a well-earned appointment with my bed…

NARRATOR. Scrooge left his counting house, and stepped out into the bracing cold air.

(SFX: DOOR OPENS, LOCK, PLUNGER WIND)

SCROOGE. Whoo. It's cold.

(SFX: DOOR SLAM, PLUNGER WIND UP, NIGHT TIME LONDON AND SNOW STORM)

NARRATOR. Scrooge left his counting house, and stepped out into the bracing cold air.

*(Noticing **ST. CLAIRE** changing costumes he has pulled from his trunk, **CLIFTON** moves to the center mic and tries to cover St. Claire's wardrobe change.)*

But before he stepped outside, he put on an overcoat. And he put it on very slowly. V-e-r-r-r-y slowly, indeed. Almost too slowly in fact…and then, he put on a top hat, costumes not normally worn in radio, but nonetheless…

*(**ST. CLAIRE** is finished, now wrapped in heavy outer wear, moves to the center mic and waves **CLIFTON** off, annoyed.)*

Finally, we hear the sounds of the streets of London…

(SFX: BELL CHIMES 11 [ORCHESTRA BELL AS FROM A DISTANT CHURCH])

(after first chime)

…one hundred years ago today…

(after third chime, all overlapping, all Cockney:)

WOMAN (JUDITH). Christmas cakes, fresh tasty bread…

(SFX: CARRIAGE WHEELS ON GRITTY STREET AND HORSE CLIP CLOPS ON SNOWY COBBLE-STONES, ETC.)

MAN (FRITZ). Chimney sweep, chimney sweep…

WOMAN (MARGIE). Six bunches a penny, sweet blooming lavender…

WOMAN (SALLY). The finest French thread, my mum's French thread.

MAN (CHOLLY). Ribs of beef, and nesselrode pie…

*(All look at **CHOLLY**. **MARGIE** laughs.)*

The snow fell gently on the darkened London streets.

(SFX: A DOG BARKS)

The jingle of sleigh bells…

(SFX: SLEIGH BELLS)

And the clip-clop of horses…

(SFX: COCONUT CLIP CLOPS, CARRIAGE WHEELS, SCUFFLE OF CHILDREN'S FEET, CRACKLE OF BONFIRE)

(MUSIC: "DECK THE HALLS", X/W DARK MUSIC)

NARRATOR. Ah! (**SCROOGE** *adds grunts, words, and sounds to echo Clifton's description*). What a tight-fisted hand-at-the-grind-stone was Scrooge; a squeezing, wrenching, grasping, scraping, clutching, covetous old goat…a greedy, miserable old sinner, on his way to his own home where he looked forward to spending a nice quiet night…alone.

SCROOGE. This blizzard. I'll *never* get home.

(SFX: SCHOOL HAND BELL)

(MUSIC: STREET BRASS BAND "PLAY" GOD "REST YE MERRY GENTLEMEN" [THE ACTORS THEMSELVES IMITATE A SOUR BRASS BAND WITH THEIR MOUTHS] PLAYING A SHAKY BUT

*EFFECTIVE "GOD REST YE..." THROUGH THE
LYRIC "LET NOTHING YOU DISMAY")*

SCROOGE. Oh, no! Stop that racket!! Go back to your homes, you're creating a nuisance! I hope your lips freeze on your horns!

(MUSIC: BAND "DEFLATES")

POOR BOY (JACKIE). Tuppence for the poor, guv'na?

SCROOGE. I'll give you tuppence. Take that!

(SFX: STRIKING FACE)

POOR BOY. *(cries)* Aw!

(SFX: BOY FALLING DOWN)

(**BOY** *wimpers.*)

Ohhhhhhhh.

SCROOGE. Get off the streets and get a job, all of you! Unitarians. Humbug. I'll just turn down this alleyway.

(SFX: DEEP SNOW WALKING. PLUNGER WIND.)

Mmmmm.

(SFX: STOPS WALKING)

The snow is much deeper here than I imagined.

(**BUZZ** *does not expect this line.*)

(SFX: DEEPER SNOW WALKING.)

And what about the wind?

(SFX: ADDS PLUNGER WIND.)

It's got to be a wind of epic proportions. *(shouts)* This is *drama*, man!

(SFX: SWITCH TO WIND MACHINE HOWLING WIND.)

(really enjoying it) That's more like it. *(goes into King Lear)* "Blow, winds, and crack your cheeks! Rage! Blow!
You cataracts and hurricanoes, spout
Till you have..."

MARLEY (FRITZ). *(tauntingly)* Scrooooge…

(SFX: WIND SUDDENLY BECOMES VERY LIGHT.)

(MUSIC: LOW, OMINOUS)

SCROOGE. What?

(silence)

Who is that?

(SFX: CHAINS SHAKE)

MARLEY. *(more emphatically)* Scroooooooge.

SCROOGE. I don't know anyone by that name. Go away!

(MUSIC: OUT)

(SFX: VERY FAST SNOW WALKING)

(SCROOGE *panting as he runs through the snow. He mutters under the running something about the distance to his home, then")*

(ad libs) Yes, what a night! There's never been such a night. Yes, there's my door!

(SFX: KEYS, DOOR HANDLE, MATCHING THE DIALOGUE)

(ad libs, and…) My hands are too cold…

(SFX: CHAIN RATTLING, MATCHING MARLEY'S GESTURES, THROUGHOUT)

(MUSIC: RESUMES, LOW OMINOUS)

MARLEY. Scrooooge!

SCROOGE. *(rattling the door handle)* I can't get in!!

MARLEY. Scrooooge!

SCROOGE. Who calls my name?! What do you want from me? Face me, you coward! Reveal yourself!

(MUSIC: OUT)

MARLEY. *(simply, now very close)* Scrooge.

SCROOGE. *(gasps, then, with caution)* Where…are…you?

MARLEY. Right in front of you, Ebenezer.

(MUSIC: BIG SWELL [SUGGESTION: DIMINISHED CHORD AD LIB])

SCROOGE. *(like peering through a veil,* **SCROOGE** *sees him)* Marley?

MARLEY. Yes. Your former partner. Jacob Marley.

SCROOGE. But you're dead.

MARLEY. Dead seven years ago this very night!

SCROOGE. But – you can't be a ghost. You're just something I've eaten, a little gas, some indigestion. I knew that Roquefort was off –

MARLEY. I wear the chain I forged in life. I made it link by link, yard by yard…by my own free will. You have a chain too, Ebenezer.

SCROOGE. I don't understand.

MARLEY. We wasted our lives in pursuit of money.

SCROOGE. But that's what we were *good* at, Jacob. Making money *(smiles, raises his eyebrows up and down)* lots of money…and we worked hard for it.

MARLEY. We should have spent our lives serving Man*kind*.

SCROOGE. What has Man*kind* ever done for us? Man*kind* is a scheming lot, willful, greedy, lazy…

MARLEY. You have yet but one chance to 'scape my fate. You will be haunted by Three Spirits.

(Offstage sound of toilet flush. **CHOLLY** *enters with newspaper, all glare at him, he retreats, shamed.)*

SCROOGE. Jacob.

MARLEY. Without their visits, you cannot hope to shun the path I tread. Expect the first tomorrow, when the clock strikes "twelve."

SCROOGE. Jacob.

MARLEY. Ebenezer, remember what has passed between us!

(SFX. RUSTLE OF THE GHOST AND ITS CHAINS)

(MUSIC: CONCLUDING CHORD)

NARRATOR. And with that, he disappeared in a flash of light.

(SFX: **BUZZ** *PULLS OUT A BROWNIE CAMERA AND FLASH AND IN TRYING TO FLASH IT, IT GOES OFF IN HIS FACE, BLINDING HIM FOR A MOMENT)*

ST. CLAIRE. *(to* **FRITZ***)* Very good, but you sounded Welsh.

CLIFTON. *(over-enunciating to* **ST. CLAIRE***)* Mic-ro-phone. *(rescuing the show, now speaking in mic)* We'll be right back to Nash-Kelvinator's production of "A Christmas Carol" after some holiday cheer from Toots and The Boutonnieres.

(During song **CLIFTON** *speaks with* **ST. CLAIRE***, who waves him off.)*

(MUSIC: **TOOTS** *GIVES CUE NOTE AND CONDUCTS "CAROL OF THE BELLS")*

COMPANY. *(sings)*
HARK! HOW THE BELLS
SWEET SILVER BELLS
ALL SEEM TO SAY,
"THROW CARES AWAY."
CHRISTMAS IS HERE
BRINGING GOOD CHEER
TO YOUNG AND OLD
MEEK AND THE BOLD

DING, DONG, DING, DONG
THAT IS THEIR SONG
WITH JOYFUL RING
ALL CAROLING
ONE SEEMS TO HEAR
WORDS OF GOOD CHEER
FROM EV'RYWHERE
FILLING THE AIR

HARK HOW THE BELLS
SWEET SILVER BELLS
ALL SEEM TO SAY
"THROW CARES AWAY."
GAILY THEY RING

WHILE PEOPLE SING
SONGS OF GOOD CHEER
CHRISTMAS IS HERE
MERRY, MERRY, MERRY, MERRY CHRISTMAS
MERRY, MERRY, MERRY, MERRY CHRISTMAS
CHRISTMAS IS HERE, CHRISTMAS IS HERE
CHRISTMAS IS HERE, CHRISTMAS IS HERE
CHRISTMAS IS HERE, CHRISTMAS IS HERE
CHRISTMAS IS HERE, CHRISTMAS IS HERE
CHRISTMAS IS HERE
DING, DING, DONG

CLIFTON. Now we return to Nash-Kelvinator's "A Christmas Carol" on WOV, Newark. This segment is brought to you by the makers of Nucoa Margarine.

(SFX: WIND)

SCROOGE. Marley? Marley? Didn't happen. An apparition. Simply a product of my poor digestion. Get in the house.

(SFX: RATTLE OF KEYS, LOCK)

SCROOGE. *(cont.)* Up to my flat. Rest is what I need.

(SFX: OPEN AND CLOSE FRONT DOOR, SHUT DOOR)

Safe. Whew! Home at last. Mmmm...cold.

(SFX: RUBS HANDS TOGETHER, BLOWING INTO THEM TO KEEP WARM)

*(**ST. CLAIRE** goes Upstage and removes his coat, etc., **SALLY** takes it.)*

CLIFTON. Scrooge went inside his house and climbed the many stairs to his garret flat –

*(notices **ST. CLAIRE** changing costume again, so moves to the center mic, a little exasperated)*

But first, of course, he took off his coat, because, as we all know, any coat that is put on will eventually be taken off, and that's exactly what Scrooge did.

(**ST. CLAIRE** *is finished changing, comes down to the center mic, again waving* **CLIFTON** *off, annoyed.*)

SCROOGE. Now, up the stairs…

(SFX: TWO FLIGHTS OF STAIRS. WOOD SQUEAKS AND GROANS. EACH FLIGHT, SAME ROUTINE FOR EACH OF THE TWO FLIGHTS: THREE FOOTFALLS ON STEPS, TWO FOOTFALLS WALKING ON LANDING, THREE FOOTFALLS ON STEPS, OPENING DOOR, TWO FOOTFALLS CROSSING THE LANDING, SHUTTING THE DOOR.)

(**SCROOGE** *ad libs while 'climbing the stairs', then, to* SFX *man.*)

(**BUZZ** *thinks he's through.*)

(an ad lib) One more flight.

(SFX: BUZZ DOES ANOTHER FLIGHT, BUT MUCH FASTER AND WITH ATTITUDE.)

Now carefully up this creaky ladder…through the attic door.

(SFX: SQUEAKY TWANG OF THE SPRING OF THE CEILING DOOR [OPENING AN IRONING BOARD] SCROOGE CLIMBS IN, DOORS SLAPS SHUT)

(an ad lib) Now, I'll lock myself up tight…

(SFX: LOCKS AND KEYS, FOLLOWS SCROOGE'S LIST. MOST HARDWARE IS ON THE PROP DOOR)

(**ST. CLAIRE** *ad libs to see if he can throw* **BUZZ**. *He can't.*)

First, the deadbolt lock. Then the security chain. Now the lever lock…the pin-tumbler padlock…my mortise handle lock…the crime bar…

(The list is delivered a little faster.)

the combination lock…the hasp lock, the barrel bolt… my latch guard…the cable lock…and the U-Bar lock…

(**BUZZ** *"buffs" his nails on his shirt front.*)

NARRATOR. He sat down before the fireplace…

(**ST. CLAIRE** *goes upstage to his trunk and removes a dressing gown, ad libs throughout, muttering, humming, etc.* **CLIFTON** *again improvises to cover.*)

But first, he put on his dressing-gown. It was a beautiful dressing gown…brocade and hand-embroidered. And, as always, he put it on very slowly and methodically. No one knew he had brought with him such a beautiful dressing gown. Or feel the need to change into it on this particular occasion. But he did.

(*trying to move* **ST. CLAIRE** *along*)

Then he sat down before the fireplace…

(**ST. CLAIRE** *puts on cap.*)

but first he put on a delightful nightcap.

(**ST. CLAIRE** *removes a lit candle from his trunk.*)

And of course, he lit a candle…

(*SFX: CLOTHES*)

…and sat down before the fireplace.

SCROOGE. Just one lump of coal.

(*SFX: ONE COAL ONTO GRATE*)

And now a little brandy.

(*SFX: CORK THUNKS*)

Just a teaspoonful.

(*SFX: CLINK OF TEASPOON TO BOTTLE. BOTTLE DOWN ON TABLE SURFACE. MANTLE CLOCK STRIKES 12*)

(*yawns mightily*) Humbug. Humbug. Humbug. Christmas. The worst day of the year. It will be over soon enough.

All I need is a good night's –

(*Silence. Noise from theatre lobby.*)

What's that? The first ghost? Is it Marley returned? (*dramatically*) Who is there?

(The conventioneers have returned, partying in the hall-way.)

CHOLLY. *(matter-of-factly)* It's the Shriners.

*(**CLIFTON** sprints out to the hall.)*

CLIFTON. *(off)* Hey, we're trying to do a broadcast in here!

*(The noise stops suddenly. **CLIFTON** returns, smiling weakly to the audience.)*

SCROOGE. Well. Off to dreamland… *(Soon he snores lightly.)*

(SFX: MANTLE CLOCK STRIKES TWELVE)

*(**ESTHER** slips onstage again. She carries some piece of audio equipment, lingers to listen to the show for a page or two.)*

(SFX: CLOCK TICKS [METRONOME]. RATTLE OF THE LOCKED SHUTTERS.)

GHOST OF CHRISTMAS PAST (MARGIE). Oh, the shutters are locked, guess we'll have to do this the hard way…

SCROOGE. *(waking suddenly)* What? Who? Where? The shutters are secure. The door is locked. So I am safe.

NARRATOR. Then suddenly the window broke…

(SFX: WINDOW BREAKS)

The air was filled with phantoms all moaning and in chains!

*(SFX AND **CAST**: PHANTOMS MOAN AND HOWL)*

(MUSIC: EERIE MUSIC)

*(The **CAST** improvises ghoulish howls and moaning.)*

SCROOGE. Get away! Get away!

(SFX/MUSIC: CONTINUE)

NARRATOR. Scrooge leapt into his bed.

(SFX: PILLOW)

And hid under the covers.

(SFX: THE BED COVERS FLAP)

(MUSIC: BUILDS TO SUSPENSEFUL CRESCENDO, THEN TRANSITIONS TO A CHEERY INSTRU-MENTAL OF "DECK THE HALLS", AS BEFORE)

CLIFTON. You are listening to the Nash-Kelvinator Mystery Theatre presentation of "A Christmas Carol" by Charles Dickens. This is WOV "Air Theater" in the Aberdeen Hotel in Newark New Jersey. This is the Mutual Broadcasting System.

(MUSIC: INTRO TO WOV JINGLE. BUZZ PLAYS HIGH-HAT.)

MEN. *(sing)*
W – W – W – W...
SOMEBODY STOP ME
...O – V!
W – W – W – W...
JUST TRY AND TOP ME
.. O – V!
COMING FROM DOWNTOWN NEWARK
1280 ON YOUR DIAL
THAT POWERFUL, POWERFUL STATION

MARGIE. *(sings)*
WITH THAT ONE BIG KILOWATT SMILE – HA!

MEN. *(sing)*
MUTUAL MUTUAL MUTUAL MUTUAL
MARCHING TO VICTORY
WE'RE W – W – W – W...
NO ONE CAN STOP US

FRITZ. *(sings)*
...O – V!

CLIFTON. W-O-V for victory time is 8...

(SFX: TRIANGLE)

...*[whatever the time is]*, Eastern War Time. We'll be right back with Chapter Two of Charles Dickens' "A Christmas Carol." But first, I've got a message to all you moms out there. Among the many challenges we are facing these days, there is none more tragic than the shortage of meat. And it doesn't matter if you have *100* brown ration stamps; there's just *no meat to buy with them.* You might be faced with the inconvenience of having to serve vegetables for dinner.

(**CAST** *is disgusted by the thought.*)

CLIFTON. *(cont.)* Do what we do at our house. Mrs. Feddington has found a sure way to make vegetables acceptable to our family.

(**CAST** *looks around:* **CLIFTON** *isn't married.*)

Well, we have three mothers in our studio right now who will speak for millions about Nucoa *[pron. NEW-ko]* Margarine. Mrs. Russell from the Bronx, New York.

WOMAN (MARGIE). *(with heavy Bronx accent)* Oh my Gawd… Nucoa Mahgarine is so delicious, you wouldn't believe. This stuff is bettah than buttah. And it's scientifically controlled. I know exactly what I am giving my children.

CLIFTON. Here's Mrs. W.D. Wilson, Maple Grove, Minnesota.

WOMAN (MARGIE). *(with thick Minnesota accent)* The money Nucoa saves us sure shows up on our food bills, you betcha. Nucoa is the sensible way to stretch food dollahs, doncha know.

CLIFTON. Finally, here's Mrs. Hendley of Ludowichi, Georgia *[pron. loo'duh-wee'-see]*.

WOMAN (MARGIE). *(with Southern drawl)* Nucoa is so dahgestible. So different from the old-tahm oleos.

CLIFTON. Thank you, ladies.

MARGIE. Thank you, Clifton.

CLIFTON. This delicious modern margarine fits ideally into today's "nutrition for defense" program. It enriches family meals in flavor and food energy at a low, low cost…For table use, tint Nucoa golden yellow with the pure "Color Wafer" included in every package; for cooking, use it just as it comes: pure, natural white! Nucoa, the wholesome vegetable oleomargarine.

(MUSIC: PIANO "DECK THE HALLS", SOFTLY)

Return with us now to the Nash-Kelvinator Mystery Theatre presentation of Charles Dickens' "A Christmas Carol." This portion of our program is brought to you by Lucky Strike cigarettes. Join the fight for freedom by *smoking* Luckies.

"A Christmas Carol" by Charles Dickens. Chapter Two: The Ghost of Christmas Past.

*(SFX / MUSIC: SUDDEN REPRISE OF PHANTOMS, BACK WHERE WE WERE BEFORE THE BREAK [*CLIFTON *ALWAYS "CONDUCTS" THE PHANTOMS, USING A CONDUCTOR'S BATON HE STOLE FROM TOOTS])*

SCROOGE. *(shouting, in panic)* No. No. I've done nothing wrong. Please leave me alone.

PAST (MARGIE). *(think Dame Edith Evans with haughty, upper-class accent, deeply trilled "r's," etc.)* Ebenezer Scrooge?

SCROOGE. Who are you?

(SFX: LIGHT WIND)

PAST. Yoo-hoo! Up here!

(MUSIC: LIGHT TINKLING MUSIC [SUGGESTION: ASCENDING AUGMENTED TRIADS])

SCROOGE. *(looking up)* You're floating above my bed!

PAST. I am indeed, and, it isn't easy, believe me. I am the Ghost of Christmas Past, Mr. Scrooge. May I call you Ebenezer?

SCROOGE. I suppose.

(MUSIC: GRADUALLY BUILDING)

PAST. You may rise and walk with me.

SCROOGE. I may?

PAST. *(firmly)* You *will.*

SCROOGE. Why?

PAST. I will show you.

SCROOGE. What?

PAST. Yourself.

(MUSIC: MINOR CHORD. SWELL.)

NARRATOR. They passed through the wall.

(SFX: MAGIC CHIME)

*(**SCROOGE** howls like Goofy.)*

Suddenly they found themselves on a country road…

*(SFX: [**SALLY**] 4 OR 5 FARM ANIMALS, HER LAST IS A MONKEY)*

BUZZ. *(off-mic)* A monkey on a farm?!

NARRATOR. …with fields on either side.

(SFX: HORSES ON SOD, SOME OF THE CAST BEAT THEIR CHESTS WITH PLUNGERS)

BUZZ. *(distant)* Tally-ho!

NARRATOR. It was a crisp, quilt-cold winter's day.

*(SFX: [**SALLY**] DOG BARK)*

PAST. Recognize you this countryside?

SCROOGE. *(gasps)* I know this place. Every rock. Every tree. I was born in this place. I was a boy here.

PAST. And that desolate red-brick structure smothered by English ivy?

SCROOGE. Ah, that's the "prison" where I attended boarding school.

(SFX: "CHILDREN" PLAYING OUTSIDE)

PAST. Prison, indeed.

SCROOGE. There's Bobby, Dick, Mary and Tom. Dick, it is I, Ebenezer! Dick!

PAST. These are but shadows of things that have been, Ebenezer. They have no consciousness of us. Come, Ebenezer, pull back that shrubbery.

(SFX: BRUSH)

What do you see through that window in that cold, barren room?

(SFX: SQUEAKS AS **SCROOGE** *WIPES WINDOW WITH HIS SLEEVE)*

PAST. Mm?

(MUSIC: SOFT AND MOVING)

SCROOGE. I see a boy.

PAST. A solit'ry child, neglected by his family. Alone.

SCROOGE. *(sighs)* Always alone. Holidays and all.

(MUSIC: OUT)

PAST. Your lip is trembling, Ebenezer. And what is that upon your cheek?

SCROOGE. A pimple.

PAST. The other cheek.

SCROOGE. Oh, it's nothing. I just wish I – ah, it's too late now.

PAST. What is the matter?

SCROOGE. Nothing, nothing. There was a poor boy begging for tuppence last night. I should have given him something, that's all.

PAST. Oh, but you gave him something alright.

SCROOGE. Humbug.

PAST. *(a proclamation)* Let us see another Christmas!

(SFX: MAGIC CHIME)

SCROOGE. There I am, alone again. All the other boys had gone home for the holidays.

(SFX: DOOR OPENS, LITTLE PARTY SHOE FOOT-STEPS)

FAN (SALLY). *(young British ingenue, lots of pluck)* Dear, dear brother.

SCROOGE. It's Fan. My dear little sister, Fan. My Fanny. How I loved my little Fanny.

*(***CAST** *look up, realizing the double meaning.)*

All the boys at school loved my little Fanny too.

*(***CAST** *look up again.)*

Fan?! Fan?! It's me, Ebenezer.

PAST. She can't hear you, Ebenezer. Your little Fanny is only a vision of what *was*.

YOUNG SCROOGE. Fan!

FAN. I have come to bring you home, dear brother! Home, home, home. *Really* I have.

YOUNG SCROOGE (JACKIE). Home, my little Fan?

FAN. Home for Christmas. Father is so much kinder than he used to be – *really* he is; he spoke so gently to me after dinner one night – *really* he did. He only strikes me when I *really* deserve it – *really* he does when really I do.

SCROOGE. Don't believe it, Fan!

FAN. So I was not afraid to ask him once more if you might come home – *really* I did – and he said "yes," you should; and sent me in a coach to bring you.

YOUNG SCROOGE. Really?

FAN. Yes. *Really* he did. We're to be together all the Christmas long, and have the merriest time in all of the world. *(pause) Really* we will.

HEADMASTER. You!

(MUSIC: SINISTER)

SCROOGE. Our Headmaster. Pure evil. Beat me worse than my father *ever* did.

HEADMASTER. Are you leaving us now, Ebenezer?

YOUNG SCROOGE. This is my Headmaster, Fan. Headmaster, this is my little sister, Fan. She has come to bring me home.

HEADMASTER. I'm surprised that your family wants you home this Christmas, Ebenezer.

YOUNG SCROOGE. Uhhh…

HEADMASTER. Well, I suppose your father has a belt he can use to keep you in line until you return to us

SCROOGE. He scared the pudding out of my Fanny.

(MUSIC: OUT)

(CAST again react, but ST. CLAIRE is unaware of the double meaning.)

FAN. It was so very nice to meet you, sir! *Really* it was!

(SFX: DOOR CLOSES DEPARTURE IN CARRIAGE [WHIP, HORSE NEIGH, HORSES ON SOD, CARRIAGE WHEELS, ETC.])

SCROOGE. My Fan.

PAST. Such a delicate creature, whom a breath could wither.

SCROOGE. She had such a big...

(CAST *turn page of their scripts at the same time.)*

SCROOGE. ...heart.

PAST. *(an ad lib)* Yes, that too.

SCROOGE. She died a young woman, while I was away at school.

PAST. She had children, I think?

SCROOGE. One child.

PAST. Your nephew.

SCROOGE. Fred.

PAST. Whom you never see.

SCROOGE. *(suddenly sour)* The man's a fool. Doesn't have the sense God gave lettuce. Get on with it.

PAST. Let us proceed, Ebenezer. You have much to learn, but a short time for such an education.

SCROOGE. Where are you taking me, Spirit?

PAST. You will see soon enough.

NARRATOR. And they found themselves in the busy thoroughfares of a city, soon...

(SFX: CARRIAGE PULLING AROUND THE CORNER, SQUEAKY WOODEN WHEELS)

...soon arriving at a large hall where they could hear a party going on.

(MUSIC: A BRIEF BRIDGE...DISTANT MERRY PARTY MUSIC UNDER)

ST. CLAIRE. *(a little confused)* Is it the Shriners again?

PAST. For Heaven's sake no, Ebenezer, look closer. Know you this place?

(SFX: PARTYGOERS LAUGH AND TALK UNDER, GLASSES CLINKING)

(MUSIC: UNDERSCORE, "HORNPIPE" MUSIC)

SCROOGE. *(delighted)* Know it?! Know it! I apprenticed here at this counting-house! And there's my old employer! Bless his heart. Old Fezziwig! My first employer – alive again! Standing by the punch bowl. It's one of his Christmas parties! *(chuckles happily)*

YOUNG SCROOGE (JACKIE). Mr. Fezziwig?

FEZZIWIG. **(FRITZ** *turns downstage suddenly, bug-eyed)* Yesssss…

(SFX: APPLAUSE SIGNS FLASH)

YOUNG SCROOGE. A wonderful party.

FEZZIWIG. I know.

YOUNG SCROOGE. Everything is just perfect.

FEZZIWIG. It is.

YOUNG SCROOGE. And you've provided such scrumptious treats.

FEZZIWIG. We have.

YOUNG SCROOGE. I want to dance with Mrs. Fezziwig.

FEZZIWIG. You do.

YOUNG SCROOGE. She's such a lovely woman.

FEZZIWIG. She is.

YOUNG SCROOGE. Do you think she'd dance with me?

FEZZIWIG. She might.

YOUNG SCROOGE. Would you care for a punch?

FEZZIWIG. No, but you could give me a kick!

(MUSIC: FIDDLE TWO-STEP, ["HORNPIPE" MUSIC] TOOTS WITH ONE OF THE CAST PLAYING FIDDLE)

SCROOGE. Merciful Heaven. How happy I was then. Old Fezziwig! And look at this food! The tables are loaded with roasts and cider, mince pie and beer! Beer! Look at the foamy tops. Here, I want a pint myself!

(MUSIC: TRANSITION, "VANISHING" MUSIC)

(**SCROOGE** *grabs an invisible pint and blows off the head then sees everything dissolve and disappear.*)

Wait! Wait! I didn't get…my…beer…the food…the dancing…where did we all go?

(MUSIC: SPOOKY [SUGGESTION: MINOR, SAD VERSION OF "HORNPIPE" MUSIC])

PAST. Alas, these are but shadows of the past, Mr. Scrooge, so very far away from you now.

SCROOGE. Humbug.

PAST. 'Twas such a small thing for Old Fezziwig to fill you with joy.

SCROOGE. *(indignant)* Small thing, indeed.

PAST. Spending but a few pounds of your mortal money…

SCROOGE. *(scoffs)* It's not about money…

(MUSIC: SEGUE AS ONE INTO "MORAL OF THE STORY" MUSIC [MAJOR KEY])

…Old Fezziwig's power lay not in spending money, but in words and gentle looks and in things so tiny that it was impossible to count 'em up. The happiness he gave us was quite as great as if it cost a…a…

PAST. Mmm, mmm?

(MUSIC: FADE OUT)

SCROOGE. What?

PAST. Something, I think?

SCROOGE. No, no. I should like to say something to my clerk just now is all.

PAST. You've already said quite a lot, I think.

SCROOGE. Humbug.

PAST. What is a "humbug," exactly?

SCROOGE. Humbug.

PAST. My time grows short. I think you are now ready to make the most difficult journey into your past. Our last to be sure, for this will be the hardest for you to endure.

SCROOGE. *(sincerely)* No, no, no, spare me this!

(MUSIC: CRESCENDO AND OUT)

CLIFTON. You are listening to "A Christmas Carol" by Charles Dickens. This is WOV Air Theatre in Newark New Jersey.

You know, folks, the pages of American history are illumined by the doctors who have worked unceasingly to overcome disease. The makers of Lucky Strikes are pardonably proud of the standing of this cigarette among doctors. An independent research organization asked this question of 113,597 doctors, doctors in every field of medicine: "What cigarette do you smoke, doctor?" The brand named most was Lucky Strike. Yes, according to a recent nationwide survey, more doctors smoke Luckies than any other cigarette.

WOMAN (JUDITH). And remember, Clifton, that over the holidays we're going to come face-to-face with some of the richest, most calorie-filled foods known to man. Make a diet resolution today! When tempted by sweets this Christmas, reach for a Lucky Strike instead.

CAST. *(whispers)* LS/MFT. LS/MFT.

CLIFTON. LS/MFT: Lucky Strike Means Fine Tobacco. Now let us return to the centennial production of "A Christmas Carol," where we rejoin Scrooge and The Ghost of Christmas Past.

(MUSIC: CHEERY "DECK THE HALLS")

SCROOGE. Where have you brought me, Spirit?

PAST. You're now a man in his prime. Your face has begun to wear the signs of greed and avarice. And your eyes are the eager, restless eyes of a miser.

SCROOGE. *(begins to weep)* No! No, please!

PAST. *She* knows it, too – that girl by your side. I see tears in her eyes.

(MUSIC: TURNS GENTLE AND SAD, UNDER [SUGGESTION: AD LIB SOFT PUNCTUATION OF SOME OF BELLE'S PITHY LINES])

SCROOGE. *(composed, quietly)* It is Belle.

BELLE. I matter so little to you, Ebenezer. Another idol has displaced me in your heart; and if it can cheer and comfort you in times to come, as I would have tried to do, I have no just cause to grieve.

YOUNG SCROOGE. Belle, what idol is that?

BELLE. A golden one. When we were engaged, we were both poor.

YOUNG SCROOGE. Was it better to be poor?

BELLE. Better, at least, to be happy. You've a changed nature; your character has changed. I've seen your nobler ambitions fall off one by one.

*(**CHOLLY** makes an unintentional noise, **CAST** all look over.)*

You've lost everything that made my love of any value in your sight.

YOUNG SCROOGE. Belle.

BELLE. So I release you from your promise.

(MUSIC: START BUILD)

YOUNG SCROOGE. No.

SCROOGE. No.

BELLE. Oh, it may cause you pain at first – a very brief pain. But soon it will be dim, like a half-remembered dream – an unprofitable dream. May you be happy in the life you have chosen, Ebenezer.

(SFX: DOOR SHUTS)

YOUNG SCROOGE. Belle!

SCROOGE. *(sadly)* Belle. Good-bye, Belle.

(MUSIC: CRESCENDO END OF CHAPTER)

Show me no more, Spirit!! Take me home!

PAST. That these are shadows of the things that have been, you must not blame me.

SCROOGE. Spirit! Take me back! Take me back! Please! Please!

(MUSIC: CONCLUDING GLISSANDO, THEN OUT.)

(SFX: SILENCE AND CLOCK TICKING.)

SCROOGE. *(with relief)* I'm in my bed. Have I been dreaming?

(cautiously) Spirit?

(quietly) An illusion. A nightmare. Heh heh heh.

(SFX: FLUFFING PILLOW)

SCROOGE. Time for bed. Imagine. Spirits.

(After a yawn and sigh, he is asleep.)

(SFX: KNOCKING)

SCROOGE. What was that?

GHOST OF CHRISTMAS PRESENT (FRITZ). Ho. Ho. Ho. Ho.

(MUSIC: IN. [SUGGESTION: JOLLY "OOM PAH" MUSIC, IN THREE; MAJOR CHORDS OVER A DISSONANT BASS] CRESCENDO)

SCROOGE. Nobody's here.

PRESENT. Ebenezer Scrooge?

SCROOGE. He's been called away.

PRESENT. Ho ho ho ho…

SCROOGE. Get away from my door.

(SFX: POUNDING)

Oh, no, you're breaking down my door!

(SFX: DOOR BREAKING DOWN, BUZZ JUMPS ON FRUIT CRATES WEARING HEAVY BOOTS, SALLY HOLDS THE WAND MIC.)

No. No. No. No….!

(SFX: ALL OUT)

(MUSIC: BIG SWEEPY END ORGAN [SUGGESTION: MINOR SIXTH CHORD])

CLIFTON. Well, folks, it's almost time for our station break tonight. We have a special treat for you folks. Margie O'Brien is going to sing a new holiday tune for you:

"THAT CUTE LITTLE ELF"
(MUSIC: THAT CUTE LITTLE ELF)

MARGIE. *(sings)*
I'VE ALWAYS BEEN A NO NONSENSE GAL
DOING WHAT I SHOULD
BUT I'VE TURNED INTO MUSH
SINCE I GOT A CRUSH
AND IT FEELS MIGHTY GOOD
NO MORE SENSIBLE AND SELF RELIANT
THE CHANGE YOU SEE IN ME
IS NOTHING SHORT OF GIANT...

*(**BUZZ** runs in clutching a long yellow teletype sheet of paper, thrusts it at **CLIFTON**.)*

CLIFTON. *(official)* BULLETIN, BULLETIN, BULLETIN!

*(**CAST** suddenly in rapt attention. **ST. CLAIRE** too, although he is slow to realize what exactly the bulletin is. **MARGIE** is very upset. **CLIFTON** waves off **MARGIE** and **TOOTS**.)*

Fresh off the wire service of the Mutual Broadcasting System, we have just received the following front line reports brought to you by Ray-O-Vac leakproof batteries, the batteries that power the flamethrowers that are helping us crush our enemy. After Victory, the battery you will surely want is Ray-O-Vac.

(REC'G: TELETYPE)

Attacks on Berlin continued through the night with bombings of 364 Lancasters and 15 Halifaxes. German fighters encountered difficulty with the weather and were able to shoot down only 16 Lancasters, just 4% of the Allied force.

On the Eastern Front...Soviet forces launched a new offensive tonight to recover recent losses west of Kiev. The 1st Ukrainian Front penetrated the lines of the German 4th Panzer Army.

In the Solomon Islands...

(**CHOLLY**, *leaning on the turntable table, causes it to rip across the 78.* **BUZZ** *replaces the needle.*)

CLIFTON. …an American task force of cruisers and destroyers bombarded Buka Island and the Japanese base at Buin on Bougainville. We are told that these are diversionary attacks from the imminent landing on New Britain in the Bismarck Archipelago.

(REC'G: TELETYPE OUT)

ST. CLAIRE. *(upstage, from his chair)* What about France? *(telephone rings)* Any word on France, or the 9th Air Force?

MARGIE. *(cueing* **TOOTS***)* Okay, Toots.

(**ESTHER** *has entered.*)

ESTHER. *(holding the receiver)* Clifton, time for a station break. Wrap it up.

CLIFTON. *(waving off* **TOOTS***)* Now folks, buy an extra war bond every payday and send a personal message of faith and good cheer to our Allies and to all the men at the front. God bless them every one.

(**MARGIE** *is talking animatedly to* **TOOTS** *while he is trying to play.*)

*(MUSIC: BUY MORE STAMPS [***TOOTS:*** PIANO;* **BUZZ:** *BANJO;* **SALLY:** *SPOONS;* **CHOLLY:** *HIGH HAT;* **SOMEONE:** *"BASS")*

(in the manic style of Spike Jones)

MEN. *(sings)*
BUY…
MORE…
STAMPS AND BONDS
THEY ARE REALLY SWELL
CAUSE THEY BUY THE BOMBS THAT BLOW
THE AXIS DOWN TO YOU KNOW WHAT WE
    MEAN TO SAY
SO BUY BONDS TODAY
AND WE'LL KEEP OUR COUNTRY FREE!

(MUSIC: REPEATS WITH MOUTH BRASS IN PLACE OF WORDS; FIDDLE IS OPTIONAL: **SALLY** *DOES BIRD WHISTLE SFX)*

ESTHER. *(impatient, shouting over music)* Clifton!

MARGIE. Clifton!

(MUSIC: THE FINAL REFRAIN)

MEN. *(sing)*
BUY MORE STAMPS AND BONDS
THEY ARE REALLY SWELL
CAUSE THEY BUY THE BOMBS THAT BLOW
THE AXIS DOWN TO YOU KNOW WHAT WE
    MEAN TO SAY
SO BUY BONDS TODAY
AND WE'LL KEEP OUR COUNTRY FREE!

(when song is over:)

CLIFTON. Well, folks, we've gotten our marching orders from Mutual in New York. We've been given thirty seconds to wrap up this part of our program so the network can do whatever it is that they do. *(beat)* This is WOV 1280 kilocycles, Newark, New Jersey.

*(***BUZZ*** is on headset.)*

BUZZ. We're clear.

CLIFTON. Folks, while we are off the air, please do not stray far. The hotel lobby bar has a fireplace and warm drinks. Who knows, you might see a couple of us out there after the show.

(shoots a look at **JUDITH***, who is horrified)*

Right, Judith? See you in ten minutes.

Intermission

(Life continues onstage during the intermission. **MARGIE** *is furious about her song being cut.* **FRITZ** *tries to sell some shoes to someone in the front row.* **SALLY** *and* **BUZZ** *are setting effects props for Act Two.* **JACKIE** *watches* **SALLY** *and* **BUZZ** *and asks* **JUDITH** *if they are an item.* **CHOLLY** *is trying to placate* **MARGIE**. *Eventually all but* **BUZZ** *and an occasional* **CLIFTON** *are offstage. At "places," all quiets down and…)*

BUZZ. In 5, 4, 3…

CLIFTON. Hi, folks, welcome back to WOV's Christmas show. We'll be right back with the next chapter of Charles Dickens' "A Christmas Carol," but first, it's time for Toots' new tune, "A Coconut Christmas" Toots?

(MUSIC: "A COCONUT CHRISTMAS")

CHORUS. *(sings)*
IT'S NEVER, EVER CHILLY
THERE'S NOT A DOT OF FROST
AND IF YOU DREAM OF SNOWMEN
I'M AFRAID YOUR CAUSE IS LOST
IF YOU JUST WANT ORDINARY
THAT'S EXACTLY WHAT WE'RE NOT
BUT IF YOU WANT EXTRAORDINARY
HOW 'BOUT A CHRISTMAS THAT'S HOT!

CANDY CANES ON COCONUT TREES
SWAYING ALONG WITH THE MANGO BREEZE
THE GREAT BIG SKY
IS A BRIGHT BLUE TEASE
A COCONUT CHRISTMAS, IF YOU PLEASE

SANTA'S GOT SOME WORK TO BE DONE
HE AND THE ELVES, THEY ARE GETTING SUN
A GINGER TAN

THEN A SLEIGH BELL RUN
A COCONUT CHRISTMAS, LOTS OF FUN

EVERYONE ALWAYS SMILING
WATCH THE HAPPINESS GROW
IT'S THE WARMTH OF THE SEASON
BRINGING JOY BUT NEVER NO SNOW
THAT'S RIGHT, NO WHITE
BUT STILL WE ARE MERRY AND BRIGHT

REINDEER BEAMS AND PINEAPPLE SHINE
LIGHTING THE SKY WITH A RARE DESIGN
A HAPPY HEART
AND SOME SPARKLING WINE
A COCONUT CHRISTMAS, SUITS ME FINE

A HO, HO, HO, TO THE SAPPHIRE SEA
A COCONUT COCONUT COCONUT COCONUT COCONUT
COCONUT CHRISTMAS
THAT'S FOR ME
HO HO HO
(SFX: APPLAUSE SIGNS FLASH)

CLIFTON. Thanks, Toots! Toots Navarre and The Boutonnieres!

(MUSIC: CUE NOTES)

MEN. *(sing)*
"W – O – V"

CLIFTON. W-O-V for Victory time is 8 –

(SFX: CHIME [TRIANGLE])

CLIFTON. *[ACTUAL TIME]*

(MUSIC: DECK THE HALLS *SEGUE, SOFTLY)*

CLIFTON. So let's return to Nash-Kelvinator Mystery Theatre's "A Christmas Carol." Chapter Three is brought to you by BVDs. *(close to the mic)* It's what's under the pants that makes the man.

(CAST *looks around at each other.)*

(Chapter Three is a radio soap opera parody like "Ma Perkins," "One Man's Family," etc. A recap of the back story and action so far.)

(MUSIC: SOAP OPERA MUSIC, LIKE "MA PERKINS,": ORGAN WITH LESLIE VIBRATO. **TOOTS** *FOLLOWS INTENTLY, AND ATTEMPTS TO PUNCTUATE EACH NEW TWIST IN THE "PLOT" WITH A SHIFT IN MUSIC OR PULSING VOLUME.)*

CLIFTON. *(too knowing and all-too-understanding)* Well, has Scrooge at last discovered his true nature?

(A little confused, **ST. CLAIRE** *rushes to the center mic thinking he's heard his cue.)*

Will Marley's predictions come true?

*(***MARLEY*** *goes to the mic, also thinking he's been cued. Throughout, all are confused, never having heard this recap, thinking they are being called on for dialogue.)*

And what about his estranged nephew, Fred?

(Someone steps up to the mic to be Fred.)

We know that Scrooge will most likely cheat his nephew Fred out of any inheritance, and we can imagine that Fred's wife Rebecca isn't too happy about the situation.

(Someone steps up to the mic to play Rebecca. **CLIFTON** *checks his watch and the exposition gets faster and faster.)*

On the other hand, Rebecca didn't want any trouble, so she stayed out of it.

*(***CHOLLY*** *pulls* **MARGIE** *to the mic to play Lucy.)*

But Rebecca's sister Lucy got into the fray, which made Fred feel cornered, knowing how much Rebecca loved her sister, Lucy. But then Lucy went home to Farnborough at the insistence of her fiancé, Albert.

*(***CHOLLY*** *pushes* **JACKIE** *to the mic to play Albert.)*

(MUSIC: PLAY SAME MUSIC NOW, [WITHOUT SHIFTS])

CLIFTON. *(cont.)* Will Scrooge change his mind? Will the Spirits convince Scrooge to make the transformation from miser to philanthropist?

(Some **CAST MEMBERS** *come up to the mic and howl as the* **SPIRITS** *and* **CLIFTON** *waves them away.)*

After all, Fezziwig set a very high standard.

*(***FEZZIWIG*** *down to the mic)*

And what about Bob Cratchit?

*(***CRATCHIT*** *to the mic)*

Will Fan try to come to Scrooge's assistance?

*(***FAN*** *to the mic)*

And we must anticipate the tragedy of Tiny Tim?

*(***TINY TIM*** *to the mic)*

What about Fan's son, Fred?

*(***FRED*** *back to the mic)*

And will Young Scrooge's father be kinder that Christmas?

*(***SOMEONE*** *as Scrooge's Father)*

Will The Ghost of Christmas Past have even more visions for Scrooge?

(MUSIC: STARTS TO BUILD)

*(***CHRISTMAS PAST*** *to the mic)*

Will Belle return to Scrooge or is she gone for good?

*(***BELLE*** *to the mic)*

What will happen on this, the most important night of Ebenezer Scrooge's life?

(MUSIC: ORGAN SWELLS AND OUT)

Well, we'll find out soon enough as we return to Chapter Three of "A Christmas Carol" by Charles Dickens.

*(***ALL*** *are exhausted.)*

(MUSIC: CUE NOTES)

MEN, OR COMPANY. *(singing, out of breath)*
"W – O – V"

CLIFTON. W-O-V for victory time is 8 –

(SFX: CHIME [TRIANGLE])

[ACTUAL TIME], Eastern War Time. We'll be right back with the next chapter of Charles Dickens' "A Christmas Carol." But first an important message from BVDs.

(SFX: SCOOTING CHAIR BACK, CLEARING DISHES, FOLLOWING DIALOGUE)

PERRY (FRITZ). How 'bout a cigar, Tom?

TOM (CHOLLY). Naw, I gotta get goin'. Thanks for the dinner, Betty.

BETTY (MARGIE). Oh, we're glad you could come, Tom. Any time. Must be lonely this time of year, living alone and all.

TOM. Yeah, well I just haven't found the right girl yet, Betty. There's only one of you.

BETTY. Oh, look at the snow. You'll never get home in this.

PERRY. Just stay over, why don'tcha?

TOM. Well, it *is* Friday night. No work tomorrow. *(massively disappointed)* Oh, but I don't have anything with me.

PERRY. That's OK, Tom, we've got an extra toothbrush and I've got an extra pair of BVDs.

TOM. Oh no, I couldn't.

PERRY. Sure you can. Come on in the bedroom and take a look.

(MUSIC: "TRAVELLING" BRIDGE. [SUGGESTION: MODERATE "SHUFFLE" OR "SOFT SHOE"])

(SFX: DOOR OPENS AND SHUTS)

PERRY. Look at these: the costume of a sleep champion, Tom. BVD's Slumberalls: stretchy seat and stretchy knee so you can bend without bind, double thickness where it counts.

TOM. Well, don't talk as though I never heard of BVDs, Perry. I've got some on. Just look at these briefs: BVD's gift to comfort-loving guys like me.

PERRY. You're right. They're real nifty. Just look at that smart warm-brushed cotton and plush-backed waistband. They're good lookin'…

TOM. And good sleepin' too!

(SFX: OPENING DOOR)

BETTY. Hey, what are you guys doin' in here?

PERRY. I told Tom he should just stay over tonight and I was showing him my extra pair of Slumberalls.

TOM. They're good lookin'.

BETTY. And good sleepin' too.

CLIFTON. Hi, folks.

BETTY. Why, it's radio personality Clifton Feddington.

CLIFTON. Happy Holidays.

BETTY. What are you doing in our bedroom?

CLIFTON. Well, I couldn't help it, hearing all this talk about BVDs. You know, the BVD collection includes briefs, woven boxers, just look at my boxer briefs.

TOM & PERRY. Mmmm.

CLIFTON. Don't accept cheap substitutes, folks. Always look for the BVD tag hand-sewn into every garment. "Stretch…right in the seat of your pants."

FRITZ. Say, Clifton, the folks at Nash-Kelvinator have a slogan too, you know. "First you dream. Then you plan. And tomorrow it will all come true."

CLIFTON. Tell us about it, Fritz.

FRITZ. When this war is won, Nash-Kelvinator, now devoted to equipping us for fighting, will return to equipping us for living. Postwar homes will be equipped with electronic gadgetry you can only dream of. Gadgets like Nash-Kelvinator's personal entertainment center, something we call "Television."

(The CAST is mystified.)

FRITZ. *(cont.)* Yes, the time is near when *everyone* will be able to enjoy the thrill of home television.

Think of the excitement of seeing a circus parade in your own living room, the drama of a chess tournament in your den, quilting bees in your kitchen – the possibilities are endless!

When Victory comes, so will *television*.

(SFX: APPLAUSE SIGNS FLASH)

CLIFTON. Why, it's a dream come true. Really exciting. *(pause)* Of course, it will never take the place of radio…

*(**CAST** loses their enthusiasm, mutter agreement. Among them, **BUZZ** says "obviously not.")*

…but it *would* be such a wonderful addition to any living room. Put a family photo on top of it, maybe a plant, an ashtray – there's never enough space for those things…

*(**CAST** agree.)*

(MUSIC: CHEERY "DECK THE HALLS")

CLIFTON. Now we return to Chapter Three: The Ghost of Christmas Present. Brought to you by Ting!

(MUSIC: MUSICAL FIGURE)

(SFX: REPEAT OF END OF CHAPTER TWO…)

SCROOGE. No, no. you're breaking down my door!!!

(MUSIC: DRAMATIC MUSIC)

*(SFX: DOOR BREAKING DOWN, **BUZZ** JUMPS ON FRUIT CRATES WEARING HEAVY BOOTS, **SALLY** HOLDS THE WAND MIC.)*

GHOST OF XMAS PRESENT (FRITZ). Ho. Ho. Ho. Ho. Ebenezer Scrooge?

(MUSIC: PLODDING, JOLLY MUSIC)

SCROOGE. Who are you?? What do you want?

PRESENT. Ho ho ho ho…

SCROOGE. You'll pay for that door!

(SFX: POUNDING)

PRESENT. *(laughing)* Ho Ho Ho. I am the Ghost of Christmas Present! Ho Ho Ho! Look upon me! Ho Ho. I'll bet you've never seen the likes of me before! Ho Ho Ho Ho Ho Ho Ho Ho Ho Ho Ho Ho *(coughs)* …

SCROOGE. *(pause)* Spirit, where will *you* take me? If you have anything to teach me, let me profit by it.

PRESENT. Touch my robe, Ebenezer Scrooge! Touch my robe!

(MUSIC: CHORD [SUGGESTION: E7/B-FLAT])

(SFX: MAGIC CHIME THEN PLUNGER WIND)

NARRATOR. Soon, they were flying above the city, through clouds and the smoke from chimneys.

SCROOGE. *(coughing)* People burn entirely too much coal these days. It's wasteful! Layers! Wear layers, for God's sake!

(They "land.")

(SFX: ALL OUT)

SCROOGE. Where've you brought me, Spirit?

PRESENT. A humble dwelling on a humble street.

SCROOGE. But they're so… *(hard to say the word)* "poor."

PRESENT. Yet there is happiness there.

SCROOGE. Impossible.

PRESENT. Look closer.

SCROOGE. Who – who are these people? Who's that woman? And all of those children?

(SFX: SOUNDS OF FAMILY SETTING DINNER TABLE, FLATWARE AND CROCKERY. FAMILY CHATTER INCREASES UNDER FOLLOWING)

PRESENT. These are the family of your clerk, Bob Cratchit. His wife lays the table for their Christmas dinner. And that is her daughter Belinda. And their oldest daughter, Martha. And the young man with the fork in the stuffing – that's Master Peter Cratchit. The little ones, Sophie and Leo, and Baby Annie.

SCROOGE. So many children – that's irresponsible!

PRESENT. There are seven.

SCROOGE. *Seven* children??

PRESENT. *(ad libbing)* I know. I like a good cigar, too, but sometimes I take it out of my mouth.

(The **CAST** *laughs, off-mic.* **CLIFTON** *glares at* **FRITZ**, **TOOTS** *gives cue notes.)*

(MUSIC: "GOOD KING WENCESLAS")

COMPANY. *(sings)*
GOOD KING WENCESLAS LOOKED OUT
ON THE FEAST OF STEPHEN
WHEN THE SNOW LAY ROUND ABOUT
DEEP AND CRISP AND EVEN

SCROOGE. *(over the singing)* What are they singing about!? They're poor!

COMPANY. *(sings)*
BRIGHTLY SHONE THE MOON THAT NIGHT
THOUGH THE FROST WAS CRUEL
WHEN A POOR MAN CAME IN SIGHT
GATH'RING WINTER FUEL.

(Continues under, oo'ing. **JUDITH** *plays Mrs. Crachit;* **MARGIE** *plays the eldest child, Martha,* **SALLY** *plays all of the rest: Belinda, Peter, Sophie, Leo, Baby Annie – each very distinct both vocally and physically: each child is progressively shorter than the last and plays back and forth on opposite sides the stage right mic.* **BUZZ** *holds a wand mic at the floor for Baby Annie.)*

(SFX: FAMILY CHATTER UP)

BELINDA (SALLY). Here's Martha, mother!

PETER (SALLY). Martha!

SOPHIE (SALLY). Martha!

LEO (SALLY). Martha!

ANNIE (SALLY). *(into wand mic, funny, cute baby gurgling, ending with)* …DADDEE.

(excited chatter)

MRS. CRATCHIT (JUDITH). Why, bless your heart alive, Martha, my dear, Merry Christmas to you!

MARTHA (MARGIE). Merry Christmas, Mother! And my darling little Sophie and Baby Annie!!

BELINDA. Merry Christmas, Martha!

PETER. *(maybe has a cold)* Merry Christmas, Martha!

SOPHIE. *(maybe with a watery lisp)* Merry Christmas, Martha!

LEO. *(maybe has a baby "r")* Merry Christmas, Martha!

ANNIE (SALLY). *(into wand mic, funny, cute baby gurgling, ending with)* …DADDEE.

MRS. CRATCHIT. How late you are, my dear.

MARTHA. Where's father?

MRS. CRATCHIT. He's been to church with Tiny Tim. They'll be along directly.

BELINDA. *(tattling)* Mummy, Peter is sticking his fingers in the stuffing.

PETER. Mother, can't I have some stuffing?

SOPHIE. I want some stuffing.

LEO. What's stuffing?

ANNIE. (SALLY, *into wand mic, funny, cute baby gurgling, ending with)* …DUFFING.

MRS. CRATCHIT. All in good time, children.

MARTHA. *(concerned)* How is Tiny Tim, mother? Any better at all?

MRS. CRATCHIT. Sometimes I think he is. And sometimes I think – oh, dear God, if anything should happen to Tiny Tim –

MARTHA. Mother! You mustn't even *think* of such a thing!

(SFX: ENTERING THROUGH DOOR. SCUFFLE OF FEET)

BELINDA. Here's Father!!

PETER. Father.

SOPHIE. Pa!

LEO. Pa!

ANNIE. (**SALLY**, *into wand mic, funny, cute baby gurgling, ending with*) Pa!

BOB CRATCHIT (CHOLLY). Merry Christmas, everybody!

MRS. CRATCHIT. And Tiny Tim!

TINY TIM (JACKIE). Merry Christmas, Mother!

BOB CRATCHIT. Merry Christmas, Martha. Belinda, Merry Christmas. Peter, already eating the stuffing are you? Where's my little ones? Sophie and Leo! And Baby Annie?!

ANNIE. (**SALLY**, *into wand mic, funny, cute baby gurgling, ending with*) ANNIE!

MRS. CRATCHIT. And how did little Tim behave in church, Bob?

BOB CRATCHIT. As good as gold and better. (**BOB**'s *voice begins to falter*) He told me, coming home, that he hoped the people saw him in the church, because he was a cripple, and it might be pleasant to them to remember upon Christmas Day, who made lame beggars walk, and blind men see.

TINY TIM. Thank you, Father. Oh, I love church, Mother. Oh, they sang the nicest songs.

BOB CRATCHIT. (*holding back tears*) Oh, bless you, my son.

BELINDA. Are we ready to eat, Mother?

PETER. Come on, let's eat!

SOPHIE. More milk, Pa.

LEO. Pa, more milk, Pa? Pa?

ANNIE (SALLY). (*into wand mic, funny, cute baby gurgling, ending with*) NO DADDEE, MOKE!

MRS. CRATCHIT. Yes, children. We're all ready. Come, come take your places now. And, Bob, wait your turn – there's plenty! Stuffing and dressing and figgy pudding for all of you. Martha, you take care of Tiny Tim.

MARTHA. Yes, Mother. Come here, Tim.

(*SFX: SILENCE AS* **TIM** *HOBBLES TO THE TABLE ON HIS CRUTCH.*)

MRS. CRATCHIT. (**JACKIE** *"limps" down to mic.*) Make he sure he eats plenty. He's so fragile and skinny. Now, sit down, sit down, everyone!

TINY TIM. Martha, may I sit on your lap?

MARTHA. Of course you can.

MRS. CRATCHIT. Now. Shall we say grace?

BOB CRATCHIT. "Barukh atah adonoi eloheinu melekh ha-olam…" *(corrects himself, clears throat)* "Bless us, oh Lord, and these thy gifts…"

*(Flustered, **CHOLLY** drops his script, loose pages fly. Others pick pages up while the scene continues.)*

SCROOGE. Spirit! Tell me that Tiny Tim will be spared. Say he'll live.

*(**CLIFTON** cues **CHOLLY** to continue the grace.)*

BOB CRATCHIT. *(ad libbing, under)* "…which we receiveth from Thy divine generosity…"

PRESENT. I see a vacant seat in the corner, and a crutch without an owner, carefully preserved.

(MUSIC: SOMBER AND SAD)

BOB CRATCHIT. *(ad libbing, under, taking visual cues from **SALLY**, like she's playing charades)* "Bless this squash, these pickled crab apples…"

SCROOGE. Spirit, is there nothing that can be done?

BOB CRATCHIT. *(continues ad libbing, under, taking visual cues from **SALLY**)* "And even these little cloves so lovingly placed in the crab apples…"

PRESENT. If these shadows remain unaltered by the future, Ebenezer, the child will die.

BOB CRATCHIT. *(continues grace, under, cued by **SALLY**)* … these turnips and rutabagas, bless this prune stuffing, these kidneys and onions "

PRESENT. You can protect him, Mr. Scrooge. Tiny Tim's greatest trial is not far away.

CHOLLY. And this big fat goose…

SCROOGE. But how can I protect him from such a trial? I am but a man. Is harm to come to him?

BOB CRATCHIT. *(under,* **SALLY** *is rubbing her tummy)* "…and most of all, of course, please bless the Nesselrode pie!"

PRESENT. Alas, we speak of his future, the details of which I know not.

(MUSIC: SEGUE AS ONE INTO A "RELIGIOUS CHORALE")

BOB. *(finishing grace)* Amen.

MRS. CRATCHIT. Amen.

MARTHA. Amen.

BELINDA. Amen.

PETER. Amen.

SOPHIE. Amen.

LEO. Amen.

ANNIE. *(***SALLY***, into wand mic, funny, cute baby gurgling, ending with)* OKAY!

(MUSIC: OUT)

TINY TIM. God bless us every one!

(MUSIC: RESUMES, A DARKER TURN)

PRESENT. Look on this family, Mr. Scrooge, and look with a more charitable eye. No, they are not a handsome family; they are not well-dressed; their clothes are threadbare; their shoes are far from Florsheims…

CHOLLY. *(putting his script back together, off-mic)* Enough with the Florsheims already!

PRESENT. …Yes, the Cratchits very likely know the inside of the pawnbroker's shop.

(MUSIC: SEGUE AS ONE INTO SENTIMENTAL MUSIC)

PRESENT. But, they are happy, grateful, pleased with one another, and contented with the time…

(MUSIC: OUT)

SCROOGE. Spirit. What will happen to Tiny Tim?

PRESENT. My life upon this globe ends tonight in but a few moments.

(SFX: CLOCK STRIKES TWELVE)

SCROOGE. Oh, no, no. Not yet! Not yet!

(MUSIC: TRANSITION MUSIC)

SCROOGE. There – there – there are still more things I wish to learn.

PRESENT. *(fading away)* These things you will learn from still another Spirit. Still another Spirit, Ebenezer.

(MUSIC: CROSSFADE INTO "DECK THE HALLS")

CLIFTON. We will return to WOV's Charles Dickens' "A Christmas Carol" after this important announcement from the Acno Corporation.

BOY (JACKIE). Gee, my complexion's so bad I hate to even go out.

CLIFTON. Don't be such a square, Jackie. Buy Ting.*

*(MUSIC: **TOOTS**. [CHOLLY IF NECESSARY] PLAYS THE HIGHEST "G" ON PIANO [OR, IF CHOLLY, ON XYLOPHONE] EACH TIME CLIFTON SAYS "TING"*)*

BOY. Ting?

CLIFTON. Ting.*

*(At first, **CLIFTON** is pretty proud of the musical punctuations, smiles as he anticipates them, but soon he starts waving **CHOLLY**/**TOOTS** off to stop them, but they ignore him. The **CAST** gives **CHOLLY**/**TOOTS** the thumbs up to indicate that it's going very well.)*

The faster way to clear up pimples.

BOY. Ting!

CLIFTON. Ting.*

BOY. How does it work?

CLIFTON. Boys and girls have overactive oil glands. Excess oil clogs pores, and causes pimples.

BOY. Boy, I'll say!

CLIFTON. Ting* blots up oil faster, more completely than any other product of its kind. That's right, in laboratory tests, Ting* completely absorbed oil in 15 minutes!

BOY. Wow.

CLIFTON. Yes, Ting* dries up pimples more effectively than *any* other product tested.

BOY. How?

CLIFTON. Applied at bedtime, Ting*

*(waves off **TOOTS**/**CHOLLY**, who is now getting into the joke, egged on by the **CAST**)*

dries to an oil-absorbing, non-staining yellow powder that clings all night. Ting* helps *heal* all varieties of pimples on your face, chest and back. So don't let pock marks and scarring of pimples and blemishes spoil your fun. Get Ting.*

BOY. *(**CAST** is now laughing silently. **JACKIE** plays along.)* What's it called again?

CLIFTON. Ting.*

BOY. Ting?

CLIFTON. T-I-N-G. Ting.*

BOY. Ting.

CLIFTON. *(reverently)* This announcement from the Acno Corporation is brought to you as a public service.

*(**TOOTS**/**CHOLLY** does one last "ting," the highest "c" on the keyboard/xylophone.)*

(MUSIC: CHEERY CHRISTMAS TRANSITION)

Return with us now to the Nash Kelvinator Mystery Theatre production of Charles Dickens' "A Christmas Carol." Chapter 4, the Ghost of Christmas Future.

NARRATOR. Scrooge blinked once and the ghost had vanished.

(SFX: MAGIC CHIME)

Again Scrooge found himself in his bed, and lifting up his eyes, beheld the third Spirit…

(MUSIC: EXOTIC, ALMOST EGYPTIAN [SUGGESTION: PUNCTUATE SALLY'S AD LIBBED MOVEMENTS])

*(**SALLY** enters from upstage door, foot and leg first, Isadora Duncans her way downstage to the stage left mic.)*

NARRATOR. *(cont.)* …a solemn Phantom, shrouded in black, draped and hooded, coming towards him. This Phantom floated about, slowly and silently, like a green mist along the ground.

*(**SALLY** picks up an electric fan and positions it in front of her face.)*

SCROOGE. I know you. You are the Ghost of Christmas Yet-To-Come. You'll show me the shadows of things that are yet to be? Answer me, Spirit, Ghost of the Future!

*(**SALLY** turns on the fan. There is sounds of electrical arcing and the stage lights brown out, then to "darkness.")*

ALL. Esther.[*]

*(There is a mad scramble as **ESTHER** unplugs the fan in the spaghetti cluster of cords, replugs the adapter plugs and extension cords upstage center.[**])*

SCROOGE. Spirit? Spirit? *(ad libbing)* Is there a Spirit in the house?

*(The lights come back up as **ESTHER** stands there holding the cluster of plugs.)*

Why don't you speak to me, Spirit? I fear you more than any specter I've seen.

FUTURE. *(**SALLY** turns on the fan in front of her face blowing toward her, not the mic. Her voices pulses with the fan.)* I am here.

SCROOGE. I know your purpose is to do me good, and as I hope to live to be another man from what I was, lead on. Lead on! The night's waning fast, and time's precious.

---

[*] If there is no Esther in the production, All say "Clifton".
[**] If there is no Esther in the production, Clifton will do the business.

FUTURE (SALLY). *(still speaking through the electric fan)* I will lead you to a future, Scrooge. And 'tis a most fearful future, without a doubt.

(SFX: MAGIC CHIMES)

NARRATOR. Scrooge slowly took her hand. They found themselves in a church yard in the dead of night!

(SFX: OWL)

(MUSIC: **TOOTS** *PLAYS CUE NOTES FOR "SILENT NIGHT")*

COMPANY. *(sings)*
SILENT NIGHT
HOLY NIGHT
ALL IS CALM...

*(***ST. CLAIRE*** *is singing, if tentatively.* **BUZZ** *carefully removes* **ESTHER** *from the cluster of adapters.)*

...ALL IS BRIGHT
'ROUND YON VIRGIN
MOTHER AND CHILD
HOLY INFANT SO
TENDER AND MILD
SLEEP IN HEAVENLY PEACE

*(***ST. CLAIRE*** *sings)*

SLEEP IN HEAVENLY...PEACE

(They continue, oo'ing under, or use handbells.)

(SFX: CRICKETS, OWLS. The company all pull out men's combs and run their thumbs down the tines to make cricket sounds while BUZZ and SALLY do the owl sounds.)

CLIFTON. The cemetery was overrun by grass and weeds, choked with too many coffins – desolate, lonely, crumbling gravestones

SCROOGE. Spirit! Before I draw nearer to that gravestone, answer me one question. Are – are these shadows of things that will be, or – or are they shadows of things that *may* be, only?

FUTURE. Come this way, Mr. Scrooge.

SCROOGE. *(really starting to believe what he says he sees)* Who are these people? Whose gravestone are they looking at?

NARRATOR. The Spirit lifted Scrooge above the huddled multitude.

(Coarse and derisive laughter. Overlapping)

MAN 1 (CHOLLY). *(a Cockney)* Well, what do you know, the old skinflint finally kicked the bucket, eh?

WOMAN (MARGIE). *(a Cockney)* Served 'em right, the bugger.

MAN 2 (FRITZ). *(a Cockney)* Right here, Mrs. Dilber. Thought of no one but 'emself 'e did.

MAN 1. If I could raise 'em from the dead, I'd give 'em one swift kick, and I don't need to tell you where.

WOMAN. Why, what was the matter with him? I thought he'd never die.

MAN 1. *(yawning)* Gawd knows.

MAN 2. What has he done with 'is money?

WOMAN. He 'asn't left it to me. That's all I know.

(They laugh.)

It's likely to be a very cheap funeral, for upon my life I don't know of anybody to go to it. Suppose we make up a little party and volunteer?

MAN 2. I don't mind going if a lunch is provided.

(They laugh.)

SCROOGE. This is my grave, isn't it, Spirit?

(MUSIC: SOMBER MUSIC, SLOW [SUGGESTION: LOW, MINOR KEY VERSION OF SILENT NIGHT])

They speak of me in these callous words? No, Spirit! Oh no, no! Spirit, hear me. I am not the man I was. Why show me this, if I am past all hope?

(MUSIC: SEGUE AS ONE INTO A "HOPEFUL" CHORALE)

I will honor Christmas in my heart, Spirit, and try to keep it all the year. I will live in the Past, the Present, *and* the Future. The Spirits of all three shall thrive within me. I will not shut out the lessons that they teach. Oh, tell me I may sponge away the writing on this stone!

FUTURE. Follow me to another place, Mr. Scrooge, a place you have been before.

(MUSIC: SINGLE-NOTE VERSION OF ALL THROUGH THE NIGHT *IN THE KEY OF F; PIANO OR VIOLIN)*

SCROOGE. Spirit! Why have you brought me here again? Here to Bob Cratchit's home? But it's not the same – why is it so very quiet here?

MRS. CRACHIT. I have known you to walk with Tiny Tim upon your shoulder, very fast indeed, Robert.

PETER. And so have I, Father. Often.

SOPHIE. And so have I.

BOB CRACHIT. But he was very light to carry, and we loved him so, that it was no trouble. *(weeping)* Oh, my son. My little son. Tiny Tim. I loved him so.

SCROOGE. No, Spirit, tell me they have not outlived their son. How can anyone bear such heartbreak? I can tell you, Spirit, that no one can. It is impossible to fathom, impossible to comprehend. A parent's reason for living is his child.

(MUSIC: "ALL THROUGH THE NIGHT")

BOB CRATCHIT. *(sings)*
SLEEP MY CHILD, AND PEACE ATTEND THEE
ALL THROUGH THE NIGHT
GUARIDAN ANGELS GOD WILL SEND THEE
ALL THROUGH THE NIGHT

COMPANY. *(sings)*
SOFT THE DROWSY HOURS ARE CREEPING,
HILL AND VALE IN SLUMBER SLEEPING,
GOD HIS LOVING VIGIL KEEPING
ALL THROUGH THE NIGHT

(They continue, oo'ing the melody.)

FUTURE. Tim. Tiny Tim –

ST CLAIRE. No, Spirit. I can't bear it. The loss of a son is an unspeakable sorrow, an unforgiveable crime. Did not they care for Tiny Tim enough? (**ST. CLAIRE** *is now off-script)* A son is a gift that grows more precious with the passing of time. Its loss is unbearable.
David.

*(***TOOTS*** *cuts off the actors. All watch* **ST. CLAIRE**, *riveted by his emotional outburst.)*

Although you may have outgrown my lap, you never outgrew my heart. I knew you'd never return to me… *(his hands are shaking)* Can not all things be forgiven, all things reversed…? Tell me that time can be stopped and reversed and the unthinkable be prevented. Tell me Spirit. I beg you!

*(***ST. CLAIRE*** *is weeping.)*

(There is much concern about **ST. CLAIRE***'s ability to continue with the performance. While the commotion regarding what to do continues,* **BUZZ** *comes downstage and puts his arm around* **ST. CLAIRE***'s shoulder and gently leads him away from the microphone.)*

CLIFTON. *(picking up the pieces, thinking on his feet, the* **CAST** *hanging on his every word)* Overwhelmed by emotion… Scrooge was unable to continue… He needed help and he needed help fast… If Tiny Tim was to survive, Scrooge needed to make some changes, and make them quickly. He wracked his brain to think of a way that Tiny Tim could be spared…

CHOLLY. *("lightbulb")* There was only one way out: enter Rick Roscoe…

(MUSIC: **TOOTS** *VAMPS ON THE "RICK ROSCOE" THEME SONG; FILM NOIR, JAZZY STYLE.)*

CHOLLY. …the wisecracking, hard drinking, hardboiled private detective, star of WOV's "The Man With No Tomorrow"

FRITZ. Friday nights at 8.

CLIFTON. Rick Roscoe, in the most dangerous caper of his career: "The Kidnapping and Rescue of Tiny Tim."

(MUSIC: FINAL DRAMATIC CHORD. OUT)

(The **CAST** *is staring, slack-jawed at* **CLIFTON***, who shrugs his shoulders like, "It's the best I could do…" The* **CAST** *wastes no time; they jump into action immediately.)*

RICK. Where am I? Why, this appearsh to be a Pennshylvania mining town about 50 miles shouth of Pittshburgh. There's a terrible thundershtorm.

(SFX: THUNDER, RAIN)

*(***RICK*** now wears a fedora.)*

CLIFTON. We join Rick as he wakes up face down in a ditch.

RICK. I've got a jackhammer headache and a lump on my head the shize of a camel'sh hump. *(groans awake)* Cheese and crackersh, where am I?

(SFX: THUNDER, RAIN)

How long have I been down for the count? Oh, my head. I've got to get out of this shtorm.

(SFX: BEAR RUSTLES IN THE BRUSH)

What was that?

(SFX: BEAR GROWLS [INTAKE OF AIR INTO A COFFEE CAN])

No! No! It's a bear, uncommon in this mining town near Pittsburgh, but nonetheless – and he looks hungry! Get away from me, you big palooka.

(SFX: GROWLS MORE FIERCELY)

Arghh! TAKE THAT!

(SFX: GUNSHOTS, BEAR FALLS DOWN AND "DIES")

Sherves you right… *(with almost a chuckle)* I mean, really, a bear in the woodsh…? *(shakes his head disgustedly)*

(SFX: BABY RATTLE)

RICK. *(cont.)* Oh no. It'sh a rattlah. Also unheard of in thish part of Pennshylvania.

(SFX: HISSING AND RATTLING)

I'll take him out with my whip.

(SFX: WHOOSHES AND LOTS OF SLAPSTICKS. SNAKE FALLS DOWN AND "DIES")

No more wriggling for you, pal. Ya might want to look into a future in belts…

(MUSIC: ROSCOE MUSIC RESUMES)

Hey, Shpirit. Looks like there'sh a cabin up ahead. Good thing you can float, Shishter. I gotta walk through this muck. My brand new Florsheim cap-toe men'sh brown dressh shoesh, "no finer expression of shoe styling anywhere."

(CLIFTON *looks at him.* **ROSCOE** *cuts off* **TOOTS.***)*

(SFX: SQUISHY WALKING)

(back to mic) Ah…Cabin B-13. Shafe at lasht.

(SFX: DOOR KNOCK)

(SFX: STILETTO HEELS INSIDE. DOOR OPENS)

KITTY (MARGIE). *(a chorine)* Welcome to Cabin B-13 *["thoi-teen"]*

NARRATOR. At the door was Kitty Muldoon. Roscoe got an eyeful.

MUSIC: KITTY MULDOON THEME [SUGGESTION: 1940S "FEMME FATALE" MUSIC, ALMOST A STRIPTEASE])

RICK. *(into a Campbell's soup can)* She wash the kind of dame who could make your kneesh weak and your teeth chatter.

(SFX: TEETH CHATTER)

KITTY. Follow me. And walk this way.

(SFX: STILETTO HEELS CROSS THE ROOM)

RICK. *(into the soup can)* We followed, but only *she* could "walk that way"…Hummana hummana.

KITTY. Make yourself comfortable. My boss will be right with you.

RICK. Thanks, shister, but I'd rather take a gander down these shtairs.

KITTY. Suit yourself, buster.

(SFX: GOING DOWN GRITTY CONCRETE STEPS)

RICK. Hello??

*(***BUZZ*** *repeats the ends of Roscoes's words like an echo.)*

BUZZ. Hello, hello, hello…

RICK. Hello??

BUZZ. Hello, hello, hello…

RICK. Little Tim?

BUZZ. Tim, Tim, Tim…

RICK. Are you here?

BUZZ. Here, here, here…

NARRATOR. There was no answer.

BUZZ. No answer, no answer, no answer…

*(***SALLY*** *scolds* ***BUZZ*** *for his gaffe.* ***BUZZ*** *is contrite.* ***FRITZ*** *looks to* ***TOOTS*** *for an idea.* ***TOOTS*** *points to* ***CHOLLY*** *for an idea.* ***CHOLLY*** *has had another "lightbulb" and turns downstage to reveal:)*

(SFX: A SQUEAKY DOOR OPENS)

RUDOLF. *(wearing a little Hitler moustache)* Velcome to my underground home.

RICK. Now *you* look familiar.

(MUSIC: SINISTER BUMPER/STINGER)

RUDOLF. I don't think we've met.

RICK. Rick Roshcoe, Private Eye.

RUDOLF. Fridays at 8:00?

RICK. Yesh.

RUDOLF. I love your show.

RICK. Thank you. And you?

> (**RUDOLF** *hurls out long, growly, pidgin German full of spitting and obnoxioius gutteral consonants. The last word he says is "Rudolf.")*

RICK. Uh.

RUDOLF. *(a translation)* You can call me Rudolf.

RICK. Like the reindeer?

RUDOLF. You're a tool, Roscoe.

RICK. Well, Rudolf, I met your moll upstairsh. She told me to come on down. She'sh quite the lookah.

RUDOLF. Yeah, Fräulein's got some great gams.

RICK. Yeah, I'd like a chance to get my mittsh on those shtems.

RUDOLF. Forget it, Roscoe…Heinz!?! *(lots of pidgin German)*

HEINZ. Ya!

> *(jumps in air for an aerobic "attention")*
>
> *(MUSIC: MATCH WITH A MUSICAL STAB)*
>
> *(more gibberish, then)*

RICK. *(talking into the soup can)* Who ish thish guy? What's a Fräulein? And who is thish Heinz?

RUDOLF. Go over zere and varm yourself by zee fire, Roscoe, vile my associate und I make Germany great again.

RICK. Take your time, Doc.

> *(SFX: WALKING ACROSS WOOD FLOOR, CELLOPHANE FIRE)*
>
> *(MUSIC: SEGUE INTO MARTIAL UNDERSCORING)*

RUDOLF & HEINZ. *(sing)*
DEUTSCHLAND, DEUTSCHLAND ÜBER ALLES, UBER ALLES
    IN DER WELT…

RICK. Thish crackling fire is good medichine for my cold bonesh.

RUDOLF. *(conspiring with Heinz, much derisive laughter, in pidgin German)* He's such a tool, this Roscoe. Have you got your gun?

HEINZ. Is Goebbels a Nazi?

(MUSIC: OUT)

(They laugh, then)

RUDOLF. *(with little salute, simply)* Heil?

HEINZ. *(returns the salute, simply)* Heil.

*(**RUDOLF** and **HEINZ** suddenly poker-faced)*

RICK. Shay, Doc…you look familiar. Lishen.

RUDOLF. No you listen, Mr. Bigshot Gumshoe. *(more pidgin German)* Take zat…

(SFX: A PUNCH AND BODY FALLS)

*(**RICK** groans.)*

And take zat –

(SFX: ANOTHER PUNCH, A KICK TO THE STOMACH)

*(**RICK** groans.)*

And now how about this, Mr. Yankee Doodle Dick!

(SFX: ANOTHER PUNCH, HIT, A FIGHT ENSUES.)

(MUSIC: UNDERSCORE TO FIGHT)

*(**RICK** and **RUDOLF** ad lib vocally under, matching **BUZZ**'s animated and exhausting fight. The fight has taken its toll on **BUZZ**.)*

RUDOLF. Give it to him, Heinz!

*(**HEINZ** grunts some pidgin German too while slapping **RICK** repeatedly.)*

Heinz, give him all 57 varieties! Look out, Heinz!

*(SFX: FOLLOW FIGHT CLIMAX. BIRDIE TWEETS WHEN **HEINZ** GOES DOWN.)*

*(**RICK** does a roundhouse and punches **HEINZ** in the face.)*

(SFX: CARTOON FIGHT NOISES, SLIDE WHISTLES, BIRD CHIRPS, ETC.)

RICK. *(getting the upper hand)* Ooof! Ah hah! I've got you now and you better shtart talking.

(MUSIC: BEGIN CRESCENDO)

RUDOLF. *(throat as if constricted)* No, no, get your foot off of my windpipe – I can't breathe.

RICK. Talk, you!

RUDOLF. No, no, you're breaking my fingers.

(MUSIC: OUT)

(SFX: SNAPPING CELERY, CARROTS, OR BREAD STICKS; THEN, BUZZ EATS ONE)

RICK. That's not all I'm gonna break if you don't shtart talking. Who'sh the dame? What are you up to? And what's in that shecret room over there?

RUDOLF. *(innocent)* What secret room?

RICK. Don't play me for a patshy. You've been eyeing that shecret room ever since I shtumbled down the shtairs.

RUDOLF. Heinz, hide the secret room!

HEINZ. *(jumping to attention, extending his arms between* **ROSCOE** *and* **RUDOLF** *as if blocking the door)* Ja.

(MUSIC: CAPTURES HEINZ'S MOVES)

RICK. Shpirit. Show me the shecret room.

FUTURE. Look. The secret room.

(MUSIC: FOLLOWING DRAMA OF FIGHT)

RICK. That one! Ha ha ha! Now unlock the door, Rudy, before I ushe your head as an ashtray!

RUDOLF. Over my dead carcass.

RICK. Unlock the door.

RUDOLF. Over *your* dead carcass.

RICK. Alright, Shpirit, unlock the door!

(SFX: DOOR UNLOCKS, A LONG DRAMATIC CREAK OPEN)

(MUSIC: MUSICAL FLOURISH)

TINY TIM. Help!!

RICK. It's Little Tim!! I've shaved you.

(SFX: MUFFLED BABY CRIES)

Wait a minute. You've got a baby in there, too, don't you, Rudy?

RUDOLF. *(quickly)* Nein. No baby. Vat baby? I see no baby. Heinz, hide the baby!

HEINZ. *(jumping to attention, extending his arms between* **ROSCOE** *and* **RUDOLF** *as if blocking the baby)* Ja.

(MUSIC: CAPTURES HEINZ'S MOVES)

(SFX: OPENING ANOTHER DOOR)

RICK *(opening door) Thish* baby!

(SFX: BABY CRIES LOUDER)

ALL. The *Lindbergh* baby!!

(MUSIC: STING ["TA DAH"], THEN DRAMATIC UNDERSCORING CONTINUES)

RUDOLF. *(cool, with a smile)* Get away from that baby, Roscoe, or I'll give you a taste of my heater.

RICK. Shpirit, grab the kidsh and let'sh blow this pop shtand!

RUDOLF. *(one last burst of pidgin German)* Next Friday at 8, Roscoe. *(to* **HEINZ***)* Heil.

HEINZ. Heil.

(They both jump up and click heels.)

SCROOGE. *(having recovered, back at center mic)* Give me that gun, Roscoe. I'll take it from here! Get away from that baby, *thou lump of foul deformity…*

RUDOLF. Who are you?

SCROOGE. Ebenezer Scrooge!

O Austria! thou hast the complexion of a devil thou slave, thou wretch, thou coward!

Thou little valiant, great in villany!

SCROOGE. Thou ever strong upon the stronger side!
A ramping fool, to brag and stamp and swear
Upon my party! Thou cold-blooded slave…

(The **CAST** *laughs.)*

RUDOLF. What did you call me?!

SCROOGE. You heard me, you kraut.

FUTURE. Draw nearer to me, all of you.

SCROOGE. Touch the cloak, Tiny Tim. You too, Lindbergh!
We'll fly like your dad! Spirit, three first class passages
from Pittsburgh to London.

(MUSIC: FRAGMENT OF "RULE BRITANNIA")

(SFX: WIND)

RUDOLF. I'll get you for this, Roscoe! You too, Scrooge!

SCROOGE. *(calls out dramatically)* Bahhhhhhh! Hum-b-u-u-u-u-g! *(he laughs)* We'll be home by morning, Christmas
morning! Christmas. *(echoey)* Christmas…

*(MUSIC: DREAMY TRANSITION ON PIANO
[SUGGESTION: TINKLING OF "WE WISH YOU A
MERRY CHRISTMAS"])*

(The mention of "Christmas" triggers something in **ST.
CLAIRE**.*)*

SCROOGE. Christmas…Christmas…Christmas. Christmas…
It's Christmas?

(SFX: SLEIGH BELLS)

*(***BUZZ** *gently leads* **ST. CLAIRE** *back to the microphone.)*

SCROOGE. Why, where am I?

BUZZ. You're home, sir.

SCROOGE. *(getting his bearings)* Home…

BUZZ. In Scrooge's own room,

SCROOGE. In my room. And it's Christmas morning.

(SFX: WINDOW OPENS, BIRDS CHIRP

And the sun. *(with growing enthusiasm)* The sun is shin-
ing! It's clear, and bright!

(SFX: OPENING WINDOW)

SCROOGE. *(cont.)* It's Christmas morning. A new day. Look there's a fresh new blanket of snow!! Oh, it's glorious! I'm a new man.

(MUSIC: OUT)

NARRATOR. And Scrooge soon tore through the streets, knocking on doors and windows and shouting at the top of his lungs.

(SFX: ORCHESTRA BELLS AS IF FROM A DISTANT CHURCH)

*(**SCROOGE** ad libs under, running down the stairs, outside, etc.)*

(SFX: DOWN THE STAIRS, RATTLING LOCKS, DOG BARKS OUTSIDE)

He ran all the way to Bob Cratchit's house.

(SFX: DOOR KNOCKS)

SCROOGE. Cratchit!! Cratchit!!

(SFX: DOOR OPENS)

CRATCHIT. Mr. Scrooge! *(fearfully)* You told me I had the day off, sir.

SCROOGE. Take the whole week off, Cratchit! And I'm tripling your salary. I'll bring you a hundred pounds tomorrow morning!

CRATCHIT. What's that, sir?

SCROOGE. You heard me! And that's just the beginning.

(MUSIC: "JOY TO THE WORLD", INSTRUMENTAL)

NARRATOR. *(over **SCROOGE**)* Scrooge was better than his word. This Christmas morning would be one the Cratchits would never forget.

SCROOGE. Everyone, I want you to meet the Ghost of Christmas Present! Get in here.

(SFX: DOOR OPENS AND CLOSES)

(MUSIC: FRAGMENT OF CHRISTMAS PRESENT MUSIC)

PRESENT (SANTA). Ho. Ho. Ho.

ALL. Hooray!!

NARRATOR. And the Spirit had hidden one thousand presents in the Cratchit closet...

SCROOGE. Look in the closet, Martha.

MARTHA. Come on Belinda, Sophie, Peter, Leo. Let's look in the closet.

*(The **CAST** warns against opening the closet.)*

NARRATOR. And he opened the closet door...

(SFX: FIBBER MCGEE'S CLOSET, CRASH BOX)

MARGIE. *(ad libbed)* McGee, you did it again!

CLIFTON. He did it all, and infinitely more; to Tiny Tim, who did *not* die, Scrooge became a second father. And from that day forward, it was always said of him that if any man knew how to keep Christmas alive, it was he, Ebenezer Scrooge. May that be truly said of us. Of all of us. And so, as Tiny Tim observed:

TINY TIM. "God bless Us, Every One."

(MUSIC: JOY TO THE WORLD *)*

COMPANY. *(sings)*
JOY TO THE WORLD, THE LORD IS COME!
LET EARTH RECEIVE HER KING;
LET EVERY HEART PREPARE HIM ROOM,
AND HEAVEN AND NATURE SING,
AND HEAVEN AND NATURE SING,
AND HEAVEN, AND HEAVEN, AND NATURE SING.

CLIFTON. Well, folks, we hope you have enjoyed WOV'S first annual presentation of Charles Dickens' "A Christmas Carol[4].

(MUSIC: PIANO. SLOW ROMANTIC VERSION OF "JOY TO THE WORLD")

As you know, folks, the music publishers' strike continues into its third month, and we broadcasters have had
to make some very serious compromises to our programming, only being able to use songs in the public
domain, or songs not-yet-published.

We did receive one letter from one very special listener
who praised us for last month's "Whaling Songs of the
Aleutian Islands."

(**CHOLLY** *was the one who sent the letter.*)

But Toots and his wife Faith have saved the day and
written a beautiful ballad for Judith Davenport. Judith?

*(MUSIC: **TOOTS** BEGINS TO NOODLE "QUIET
NIGHT", UNDER:)*

JUDITH. This program is being transcribed to broadcast
abroad next month for some very special fellas overseas. Tonight, we continue a tradition we started back
when we were the Mutual Manhattan Cavalcade as we
dedicate this last song to a member of the armed forces
and to his family. This week, our own Buzz Crenshaw.

(MUSIC: OUT)

BUZZ. *(starts haltingly, not really knowing what to say)* I grew
up right here in New Jersey. First graduating class of
Bayonne High. The only on-campus ice rink in all of
New Jersey. Class of '37. Go, Bees. Actually that's where
"Buzz" comes from. The Bayonne Bees. I was their
unofficial mascot. My real name is Isadore. *(anticipat-
ing a reaction)* I know.

I don't have much of a family. I was raised by my aunts,
Lulu and Gilly, and they're both gone now. I never
knew my dad. These guys are my real family, so it's
them that I am leaving next month.

(beat) Well…I guess…What better way to say good-bye
to a bunch of "mike jockeys" than on the air. And tell
them how much I…I will miss them. How close I feel
to them all. You're my little brother, big brother, little
sister, big sister, aunts and uncles…

BUZZ. *(cont.)* We could have done very nicely without this war…uh. Maybe next Christmas…

Love you guys.

(pause)

CLIFTON. The final segment of our show tonight: our dedication to Private Isadore Crenshaw. Judith? Toots?

(MUSIC: QUIET NIGHT*)*

JUDITH. *(solo)*
TONIGHT IS ANOTHER QUIET NIGHT
THE HOUSE IS CALM AND STILL
NO GENTLE GLOW IN THE FIREPLACE
NO SNOW ON THE HILL

CAN SOMEONE TELL ME IF TODAY IS CHRISTMAS?
IT USED TO BE MY FAVORITE TIME OF YEAR
SPARKLING TREES WITH CANDY CANES AND PAPER
    SNOWFLAKES
SINGING TOGETHER WITH ALL OUR LOVED ONES NEAR
AS I RECALL THE WHOLE WORLD SMILED AT CHRISTMAS
BACK WHEN WE WERE YOUNG AND LOVE WAS NEW
DARLING, HERE IN MY HEART WE'RE NOT APART
AND LOVE SHINES THROUGH
BUT IT WON'T BE CHRISTMAS UNTIL I AM HOLDING YOU

*(**SALLY** looks over at **BUZZ**.)*

COMPANY.
OOH, CHRISTMAS

*(**JUDITH** joins with the company.)*

OOH, MY FAVORITE TIME OF YEAR
OOH, MISTLETOE AND STARS THAT GLISTEN
JOYFUL BELLS BURSTING WITH YULETIDE CHEER

JUDITH. *(solo)*
I KNOW ONE DAY WE'LL SHARE A PERFECT CHRISTMAS
AND THEN WE'LL MAKE OUR SWEETEST DREAMS COME
    TRUE
DARLING,

(over company oohs)

RIGHT FROM THE START YOU HAD MY HEART,
AND STILL YOU DO
BUT IT WON'T BE CHRISTMAS
IT CAN NEVER BE CHRISTMAS

(solo)

UNTIL I AM HOLDING YOU

(company)

UNTIL I'M HOLDING YOU

(MUSIC: CONTINUES, UNDER)

CLIFTON. So that's our show for tonight. We'd like to stick around a little longer, but we all have places to go, people to see, things to do…but we'll be together again next week, when that little red light on your radio turns a deep amber. Until next week, remember to drive safely, and promise me that before your head hits the pillow at night, have a delicious cup of hot…*(last chance to make a buck)* …Ovaltine, the world-famous drugless aid to natural sleep. A hot cup of Ovaltine draws excess blood away from the brain, inviting a mental calm, conditioning the mind for sleep – naturally – a sleep that rewards you with morning energy you'll never forget. Ovaltine, a product of The Wander Company, Chicago, Illinois.

So this is Clifton Feddington and the whole gang at WOV wishing you and yours a happy and healthy holiday season. *(Feddington's trademark slogan)* "Bye-bye. And Buy Bonds."

(MUSIC: OUT)

(SILENCE)

This is WOV, 1280 kHz, Newark, NJ, broadcasting courtesy of the Mutual Broadcasting System, New York

("On Air" sign goes out)

BUZZ. *(to all, off-mic)* And we're off the air.

*(All cheer. A rush to congratulate **ST. CLAIRE**, who is practically bowled over in the rush. Lights slowly fade on*

the general bustle of everyone in the studio, lights gently returning to the flat rehearsal look.)

CLIFTON. Nice show, everyone. Mr. St. Claire, the best Scrooge anyone could imagine!

(general agreement)

ST. CLAIRE. *(to everyone)* I wanted to apologize to everyone for my very unprofessional behavior –

JUDITH. No. It was sincere, and very moving.

(All add their support.)

CLIFTON. Everyone, let's pack up and get out of here. *(looking at his watch)* We can't afford to break another hour. Let's move!

JACKIE. I gotta get home.

CHOLLY. I've gotta get over to the Weequahic. Those rolls gotta be hot or she'll send me back.

CLIFTON. Pay envelopes, everyone. Move it!

*(Everyone goes to **CLIFTON** to collect. **ESTHER** appears, helps **BUZZ** a little with the clean up.)*

BUZZ. Scripts? *(collects scripts)*

CHOLLY. *(to **ST. CLAIRE**)* Pleasure.

ST. CLAIRE. Likewise. And Happy Chanukah.

CLIFTON. Judith? How about that drink?

JUDITH. I don't know, Clifton. I'm bushed.

FRITZ. Come on Judith.

JUDITH. Fritz. Clifton. I'm tired.

CLIFTON. One drink out at the hotel bar? It's quiet out there, no one's around.

SALLY. What about The Palm?

JUDITH. Yes! Yes! The Palm!

CLIFTON. Well…uh…

(general agreement)

CLIFTON. *(resigned)* Well, sure.

(**JUDITH** *and* **TOOTS** *call out their goodbyes and well wishes. They're gone.* **CLIFTON** *exits upstage to get his coat, scarf, gloves, etc.*)

JACKIE. *(entering in full outdoor winter regalia)* Well, I'm off.

MARGIE. Night, John.

FRITZ. Come on, everyone, first round's on Cliff.

CHOLLY. Well, maybe just one.

MARGIE. We can drop you at the diner.

(They exit.)

JACKIE. *(has been waiting til most have gone)* Night, Sally.

SALLY. Night, Jackie.

JACKIE. I think I'm going to go by John from now on.

SALLY. Well, night, John.

JACKIE. I got a little something for you. *(He hands her a small wrapped box.)* You know, it being Christmas and all.

SALLY. *(really touched)* You didn't have to do that. John.

JACKIE. I ran over to Bamberger's during the intermission. Oh, you don't have to open it now.

SALLY. Thank you.

*(**SALLY** kisses **JACKIE** on the cheek.)*

JACKIE. *(uncomfortable)* Well, see you Tuesday night. *(He exits.)*

SALLY. *(calling after him)* Call me if you need your car towed or anything!

CLIFTON. *(entering carrying his coat, etc.)* You all coming? Fritz says first drink's on me.

BUZZ. Maybe. Don't wait for me.

SALLY. Or me.

CLIFTON. Okay. Now don't dawdle. We can't afford –

BUZZ & SALLY. to break another hour.

BUZZ. We know.

CLIFTON. Mr. St. Claire, I just got a call that your car is downstairs.

(**CLIFTON** *is gone.*)

BUZZ. *(helping* **ST. CLAIRE** *on with his cape)* What are you doing for Christmas, sir?

ST. CLAIRE. Well, I'll probably head down to Philadelphia to see my sister.

BUZZ. You know, I was just going to cook up Christmas dinner tomorrow, something modest, you know, Cratchit style. Maybe you'd want to join me?

SALLY. I can bring my chestnut stuffing.

ST. CLAIRE. That's very kind of you...my sister's expecting me, and...why don't you two just have a nice quiet Christmas alone, cuddle up by the fire and all that...

(Awkward pause. **BUZZ** *and* **SALLY** *look at each other, a little embarassed.)*

BUZZ. *(picking up the trunk and carrying it out)* Well, let me help you with your trunk. Amazing how much it holds, really; it's almost like magic.

ST. CLAIRE. *(to* **SALLY***)* Good bye. Happy Christmas.

SALLY. And to you.

*(He is gone.)**

ESTHER. *(to* **SALLY***)* Got a place to go for Christmas?

SALLY. *(looking in the direction* **BUZZ** *just exited)* Don't know yet.

ESTHER. Well, wherever you go, have a merry one.

*(***ESTHER** *is gone.* **BUZZ** *re-enters, chilly from the cold outside.)*

SALLY. Isadore?

BUZZ. I know.

SALLY. Not going to the Palm?

BUZZ. Nah, I got to finish up here, and then I've got a turkey to stuff.

SALLY. You eating alone?

BUZZ. My neighbor might come by for dessert later on.

---

* If there is no Esther in the production, omit the next three lines.

SALLY. Oh.

BUZZ. I've never had chestnut stuffing. Is it any good?

SALLY. You like chestnuts?

BUZZ. Yep.

SALLY. Then it's good. *(looks around)* What's left to do?

BUZZ. Not much.

(They work under the following. Lights begin to fade.)

You know, I always brine the turkey overnight.

SALLY. *(trying to find out more about his mother)* Your mom's recipe?

BUZZ. Naw, Lulu and Gilly were the cooks in the house. Seriously, in a big pan of water with a handful of salt and sugar, weigh it down with a heavy plate, cover it, and put it on the back porch 'til morning…

(They work without dialogue. Sounds from the lobby bar: laughter, glasses clinking, anticipation of the night out, talk of the snow, Christmas. Some of the CAST are singing "Good King Wenceslas." Slow fade on the action.)

(CURTAIN CALL)

(Cast re-enter and sing a "mouth brass" jazzy version of "Deck The Halls.")

(BOWS)

PROPS

Show Mics:
1. Center RCA 44BX-style mic topped w/call letters "WOV"
2. SL RCA 44BX or 84-style mic
3. SR RCA 44BX or 84-style mic

SFX Mics:
1. Boom over table.
2. Contact mics under work surface
3. Wand mic for walking and stairs

Organ / Celeste / Piano *(Stage Left)*
(can be electronic, but disguise or hide the exteriors to keep them period.)

SFX Props:
1. SFX Table with quarter-sized door on one end, a removable work surface, drawer and shelves below. On door, many locks
2. Wind machine
3. Full size plunger *(stick in trousers and blow into it for soft wind)*
4. Washers *(coins)*
5. Starters pistol *(and back up pistol)*
6. 2-pieces of flat steel bar
7. Brownie "Holiday" camera with flash and flash bulbs *(for flash effect)*
8. Window-breaking unit *(and glass panes to break: enclosed box with screen sides, nail through wooden arm that comes down on scored glass sheets)*
9. Rain contraption *(see companion video)*
10. Thunder Sheet
11. Large ring of metal keys
12. Pillow
13. Large *(2' square)* blanket with satin border
14. Portable *(small)* window unit *(opens and closes)*
15. Variety of shoes *(for the visual)*
16. Step unit *(three-step)*
17. 78-rpm turntable *(spins but doesn't play)*
18. 78 rpm records *(6-8)*
19. Coconut halves
20. Half-dozen half-length plungers *(for horses on sod, see companion video)*
21. Slide whistle
22. Old wind-up alarm clock *(doesn't have to work)*
23. Metronome for clock
24. Whiskey bottle with water in it
25. A spoon
26. Carriage wheel *(old, mounted and squeaky)*
27. Flatware and crockery for dishes *(see companion video)*
28. Radio Flyer wagon, weighted on inside, a graveled surface to pull it over *(see companion video)*
29. Sand for gritty walking surface

30. Ratchet and various locks on a board
31. Water bird whistle
32. Triangle
33. Single-Row Chinese Chimes
34. Child's Xylophone for Station ID
35. Hanging orchestral bell *(for distant church chime)*
36. Cellophane *(fires)*
37. Cornstarch in box *(walking in snow)*
38. Twigs to break for brush
39. Large cooking pan with lots of wet sponges for walking through squishy mud
40. Empty period cereal boxes *(get images from internet and apply to cereal boxes)* see companion video
41. Quill and paper *(Cratchit's figuring)*
42. Men combs *(crickets)*
43. Baby rattle *(rattler)*
44. Campbell's soup cans *(talking to self)*
45. Large Maxwell House Coffee can *(for bear)*
46. Flatware and crockery
47. Sleigh bells
48. School-style hand bell
49. Marley's chains *(lots, large long strings, like for boats)*
50. Old ironing board
51. Twang-y screen door spring
52. Fruit crates *(jump on them is breaking down a door)*
53. Celery sticks, bread sticks, carrots
54. Door creaker *(for long and short creaks)*
55. Crash box, empty cardboard boxes *(Fibber McGee)* *("sweetened" by recorded sound as if played on the 78 turntable)*
56. Pair of marching band cymbals
57. Set of hand bells for Silent Night
58. Stool for Sally to sit on near SFX area *(used for furniture moving effect)*
59. Bed clothes *(mostly a visual gag)* pillow, quilt
60. Window shutters to rattle
61. Glass cleaner to squeak as window rubbed *(rubbing a window pane with a piece of Styrofoam also works)*
62. Chattering teeth

IF YOU CAST ACTORS WHO CAN PLAY INSTRUMENTS:
63. High-hat for someone to play *(anything with a tempo)*
64. Banjo for Buzz to play *(Buy More Stamps and Bonds)*
65. Fiddle for someone to play *(Fezziwig party)*
66. Stand up bass for someone to play *(throughout, where needed)*
67. Maracas and claves for someone to play *(Coconut Christmas)*
68. Spoons for Sally to play *(Buy More Stamps and Bonds)*

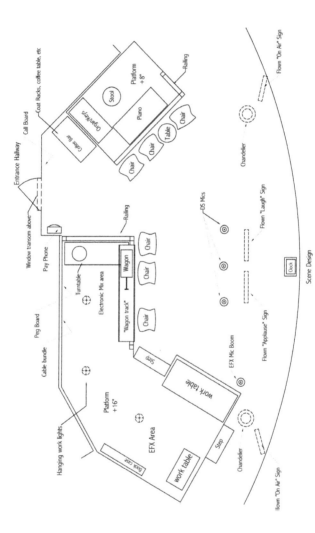

Scene Design

1940's Radio Christmas Carol

OTHER TITLES AVAILABLE FROM SAMUEL FRENCH

THE 1940S RADIO HOUR

Book by Walton Jones
Based on an idea by Walton Jones and Carol Lees
Music by various composers

Comedy / 10m, 5f / Interior

A different time is evoked in this marvelously theatrical and winning show, a live broadcast of a The Mutual Manhattan Variety Cavalcade from the Hotel Astor's Algonquin Room on December 21, 1942. The spirit of that bygone era when the world was at war and pop music meant "Strike Up the Band" and "Boogie Woogie Bugle Boy" (both are in this show) is accurately captured as the harassed producer copes with a drunk lead singer, the delivery boy who wants a chance in front of the mike, the second banana who dreams of singing a ballad, and the trumpet playing sound effects man who chooses a fighter plane over Glenn Miller. Also available in a special holiday version, *The 1940s Radio Christmas Carol*.

"Totally exhilarating hour of singing, dancing and
funny commercials."
– *New York Daily News*

"This is fun with a capital fun."
– *ABC TV*

OTHER TITLES AVAILABLE FROM SAMUEL FRENCH

A CHRISTMAS PUDDING

Edited and Adapted by David Birney

Holiday Play with Music / 3m, 3f, plus chorus 8 to 12 singers / Simple Set

A Christmas celebration told in songs, stories, poems and tales by Dickens, Mark Twain, Shakespeare, Emily Dickinson, Shaw, Longfellow,St. Luke and many others collected with a host of traditional carols and holiday songs. This piece provides a perfect evening to warm hearts, stir memories and give laughter during the holiday season.

" ...David Birney's adaptation is an evening of song, poetry and
stories that celebrate the spiritual dimensions of the season...from a
diverse array of classic and modern texts, punctuated with musical
interludes...This is definitely a Christmas show...its openhearted
sentiments send a message that's reassuringly inclusive.
–*Los Angeles Times*

OTHER TITLES AVAILABLE FROM SAMUEL FRENCH

SCROOGE!

Book, Music and Lyrics by Leslie Bricusse

Holiday Musical / Various m and f / Various sets

In 1970, renowned writer-composer-lyricist Leslie Bricusse adapted the classic Charles Dickens tale, *A Christmas Carol*, into the hit screen musical "*Scrooge!*"

Now available as a charming stage musical, *Scrooge!* has enjoyed a hugely successful tour of England and a season at London's Dominion Theatre starring the late Anthony Newly. Included are six new songs not performed in the film. Now this sure-fire audience pleaser is available in two versions: as a full-length musical and in a 55-minute adaptation that is ideal for small theatre groups and schools, where it can be performed as a short play or as part of a seasonal concert. Selected pieces from the most popular musical numbers are included in the shortened adaptation.

"If you liked *Phantom of the Opera*, just wait until you see *Scrooge!*"
– Radio 3, Australia.

"Wonderful theatre"
– *Yorkshire Evening Post*

"Sensational...it was terrific."
– BBC Radio 2.

"Here is a musical on a grand scale - a rollicking frolicking feast of entertainment."
– *The Country Border News*

"Don't miss it!"
– *Swindon Evening Advertiser*